Stories From The Vault:

A Collection of Wisdom, Illustrations, and Quips

Dr. Ronnie Williams

BURNING BUSH
BOOKS

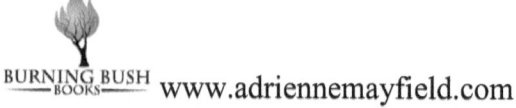 www.adriennemayfield.com

Stories From The Vault: A Collection of Wisdom, Illustrations, and Quips

By Ronnie Williams

Published by Burning Bush Books

Copyright @ 2019 by Ronnie Williams

First edition March 2019

For information about bulk purchases, please contact Ronnie Williams at ronniegbc@aol.com

Manufactured in the United States

ISBN: 978-0-9997694-4-7

All Scripture quotations, unless otherwise noted, taken from the Holy Bible, King James Version.

Cover Design: Adrienne Mayfield

Visit the author's website at drronniewilliams.org

Dedication

This book is dedicated to my daughter, Alice R. Rich, who inspired me to write this book. We go to family dinner after church quite often. One Sunday Alice said to me, "Daddy, people like to hear you tell stories. Why don't you write a book of the stories you've told over the years?" That question birthed the idea of "Stories from the Vault." Thank you, Alice, for your tireless efforts traveling with me, promoting me, and helping me promote my first book, "Sermons in Nutshells." Your contribution to the success of my first published book did not go unnoticed. Daddy loves you!

Table of Contents

FOREWORD

I like stories. I grew up sitting at the foot of my grandfather who was a prolific storyteller. Quite naturally I learned to tell and retell stories that I read and heard, and I developed a knack for crafting stories from my own experiences. When I began preaching, storytelling became a kind of trademark for me. I have been criticized for telling stories in my sermons, even in my own pulpit. A preacher came to my church once and said, "I don't have any stories to tell you; I just got a word." Needless to say, that preacher never got an invitation to come back. If Jesus the master preacher told stories in his preaching, it's should be acceptable for me to tell stories in my preaching.

In the synoptic gospels, there are many parables Jesus used in his teaching. In John, there are no parables, but all the other gospels are replete with parables. In the Gospel of Matthew, Jesus explained his use of parables. When the disciples questioned him, he answered "because it is given unto you to know the mysteries of the kingdom of heaven, but to them it is not given." Matthew 13:11. He continued in

Matthew 13:13, "Therefore; speak I to them in parables because they seeing see not; and hearing they hear not, neither do they understand." The word parable and the word parallel come from the same root. A parable is an earthly story laid parallel to spiritual truth so that people can better understand that truth.

Over my 42 years of ministry, I have numerous stories. Though I cannot remember the origin of some of the illustrations and stories offered in this book, I never forget a story. Many of these stories are not original, but many of them are a result of a creative and sometimes, runaway imagination. I wanted to share with laymen and clergy alike these tools that will not only inspire them, but will aid teachers, preachers, and presenters to be more effective in their ministry.

A Boat with No Power

During the 18th Century a steamboat was sailing on the Mississippi River, but came to a halt for no apparent reason. The captain called in the engineer and asked him what was wrong. The engineer went back to the back of the ship and checked the rudder. He examined the big turning wheel and inspected the engine, but found nothing wrong. He went back and told the captain that he could find no reason why the ship had no power.

There was a passenger on the ship that day who was a retired and revered nautical mechanic. They asked the old man to look into the problem of the ship's powerlessness. The old mechanic went to the boiler room and in a matter of minutes the ship was moving down the river. The captain asked him how he corrected the problem. The wise old man said, "The problem was not the rudder nor was it the wheel. It was not even the engine. The problem was that there was no steam because the fire had gone out in the furnace. No fire, no steam, no power."

The problem with the Ole Ship of Zion is not her programs, nor is it her budget. It is not her staff. The problem is that there is no fire and when there is no fire, there will be no steam. The Holy Ghost is the fire and joy is the steam. No Holy Ghost--no fire. No fire--no steam. No steam--no power.

Acts 1:8 But ye shall receive power, after that the Holy Ghost is come upon you: and ye shall be witnesses unto me both in Jerusalem, and in all Judaea, and in Samaria, and unto the uttermost part of the earth.

Alcohol and a Monkey's Brain

The only difference between a monkey brain and the human brain is that a human has a 1/8 inch layer of fluid around it. The human brain is literally floating in water. Experts in the medical field tell us that when we consume excessive alcohol, that layer of fluid slowly dissipates. In other words, excessive consumption of alcohol makes a monkey out of you.

Unplanned babies are conceived, lives are lost, accidents occur on the highway, health problems develop, careers are ruined, potential evaporates, brilliant minds are destroyed, and families are torn apart all because of alcohol abuse. We have to ask ourselves whether the momentary feeling is really worth it.

Proverbs 20:1 Wine is a mocker, strong drink is raging: and whosoever is deceived thereby is not wise.

Angels Watching Over Me

A few years ago, I was leaving Atlanta traveling I-75 N when I looked up and saw a sign that said 85 North. It was late at night and I was tired and paying little attention to the road signs. I am usually a careful driver, but this night I didn't signal, and I attempted to navigate my car to the left lane when it appeared that my steering wheel locked. About that time, a huge 18- wheeler came barreling alongside my car missing me by just a few feet. If I had successfully traversed my vehicle to the left lane, undoubtedly that tractor-trailer would have rammed me in the back.

On another occasion my sister called me because her car had broken down, and she wanted me to take her to work on third shift. While traveling Highway 67, around 11 o'clock p.m., I looked up and noticed there was a car in my lane coming around the curve about to hit us head-on. I only had time to utter the name of Jesus and the car miraculously went back to the other lane, missing us by inches.

I have many stories like these and I'm certain that many people reading this book have similar stories about incidences where they could have been killed. But in spite of the fact that most of us have stories like these, we are still here today. Take a look at your high

4

school yearbook, and you will discover that there are many people you played with, studied with, went to sporting events with, and sat in class beside, who are no longer here. Many of us have siblings, parents, and even children who have gone on into eternity who were victims of accidents, sicknesses and diseases or some violent act against their person. What should have killed you or could have killed you didn't. Why? You are still here. The question is why. It is because God still has purpose for you. As long as you are breathing, there is still work to do.

Psalms 91:11 For he shall give his angels charge over thee, to keep thee in all thy ways.

Angry Devil

A married couple buys a nice house and a nice car in a beautiful neighborhood, but the woman discovers that the man has been unfaithful. She takes him to divorce court and the judge awards her everything. She gets the house, the car, and half the money.

A few years later, she falls in love, and gets married again. Her ex-husband sees her and her new husband riding around town in a car that he once enjoyed. He sees her and her new partner in a house where he used to live. He knows they go to bed each night in a bed he once slept in. He becomes so angry that he wants to go crazy on both of them because the new guy has taken his place.

This is why the devil is so angry with the church. We are in a relationship he once had, but he ruined it. When our praise and worship are accepted by God, it reminds the devil of his past. He was once the worship leader in heaven but he was cast out because of pride. No wonder the devil catches an allergic reaction to our praise! Want to make the devil mad? Praise the Lord!

Isaiah 14:11 How art thou fallen from heaven, O Lucifer, son of the morning! How art thou cut down to the ground, which didst weaken the nations!

Annoying Adam

Dr. Clarence James of Atlanta Georgia told a story once of how he imagined Adam before God gave him Eve for his wife. He imagined that Adam would play with the animals all day long. They would play a game of basketball with the giraffe playing the center position. The gorilla would be the power forward, and the chimpanzee would be running at point guard. He imagined that they would play all day, but when the sun began to slip down behind the Western hills, all the animals would go home. The giraffe would go home to Mrs. Giraffe, and brother Gorilla would go home to Mrs. Gorilla while the little chimpanzee went home to Mrs. Chimpanzee. Adam would go home alone.

At midnight Adam would walk up to brother gorilla's house, knock on the door, and Mr. Gorilla would say, "I wonder who that could be this time of night." Mrs. Gorilla would say, "I'll bet you that's Adam. Tell him to go away. I don't mind company every once and a while, but I don't want nobody always sitting around me and my man."

God saw Adam was lonesome and gave him a wife of his own, and named her Eve, Dr. James concluded.

Proverbs 18:22 Whoso findeth a wife findeth a good thing, and obtaineth favour of the Lord.

Ants Need To Be In Charge

I kicked over an ant mound. Immediately they collectively started rebuilding. Not one of them looked up to see who did it. They did not form a building committee to elect a chairperson, vice-chair, and secretary. Not one ant cared what color the other one was or whether they were male or female. They didn't seek legal advice to determine if

I should be sued or not. There was no shouting, bickering, or finger pointing about who was to do what; they simply all stayed in their lane. It didn't seem that any of them negotiated a salary contract to make sure they would be properly paid and insured. They just went to work, immediately, rebuilding what I destroyed. Maybe, ants need to be in charge of America.

Proverbs 6:6 Go to the ant, thou sluggard; consider her ways, and be wise:

Atheists Will Believe One Day

The Russians were the first to go into outer space on Sputnik in 1957. When they reached their destination in the stellar reaches of space, one cosmonaut radioed back to command center and said, "We are out here in space, but we don't see God." If he would've stepped out of the space capsule, he would have seen Him for sure.

Hebrews 9:27 And as it is appointed unto men once to die, but after this the judgment:

Attractive Anointing

When God gives you an assignment, He equips you to do it by anointing you with the Holy Spirit. You have a super-natural magnetic appeal that cannot be explained in earthly terms. Some people gravitate towards you like a moth to a flame; others flee like houseflies from a fly swat. Still, there are some who attack you because of envy. It is not you; it is the God in you that they want or resist. Therefore, no progressive, anointed, or effective ministry is exempt from attacks. If you are under attack, it could be because of your attractiveness--an indication that you are on the right track. Stay the course.

John 7:7 The world cannot hate you; but me it hateth, because I testify of it, that the works thereof are evil.

Bad Kid

While flying in from Philadelphia yesterday, there was a kid in front of me on the plane who yelled at his parents the entire trip. The mother tried to appease him by walking him up and down the aisle. This was against the advice of the Captain, who predicted much turbulence on the flight as it was a really bad day for flying. She held the kid up so that he could play with the reading lights and the air vents, but he still yelled and fought her. These verses came to me.

Proverbs 23:13-14 Withhold not correction from the child: for if thou beatest him with the rod, he shall not die. Thou shalt beat him with the rod, and shalt deliver his soul from hell.

Bad Memory

A guy went to his doctor and complained, "Doc, I got this terrible problem with my memory. I can't remember a thing." The Doctor said, "Well, come on in and sit down and tell me about your problem." The guy said, "What problem?" His problem is a lot like many of ours. We are too quick to forget what God has done in our lives. A good memory makes heroes. A bad memory makes cowards.

1 Chronicles 16:12 Remember His marvelous works which He has done.

Beauty of the Lord

Want to see the Lord's beauty? Travel to Alaska and look at the beautiful glaciers, the crystal clear rivers, and towering mountains. Want to see the Lord's beauty? Go to California and look at the beautiful tall redwood trees. Travel Hwy 1 in Malibu. On one side you will see tall granite mountains and on the other side the plush blue waters of the Pacific Ocean. Want to see the Lord's beauty? Go to Texas and view wheat fields undulating under a gentle breeze. Want to see the Lord's beauty? Drive the Blue Ridge Parkway extending from Tennessee to North Carolina during fall and witness the beautiful collaboration of colors in virtually every hue; ones you cannot even find in a Crayola box. Want to see the Lord's beauty? Go look in the mirror! God did not make a mistake on you. Like the song says, "When I look in the mirror the only one there is me. Every freckle in my face is where it supposed to be, and I know my Creator didn't make no mistakes on me." India Arie *from "Video"*

Psalms 90:17 And let the beauty of the Lord our God be upon us and establish thou the work of our hands upon us; yea, the work of our hands establish thou it.

Be Careful Of Your Company

A man was driving across a bridge when he saw a guy standing on the railing preparing to jump. He pulled his car over and said to the man, "Mister, please don't jump, you have so much to live for. Don't take your life like this." The melancholy fellow said, "I have nothing to live for. I've lost my job; my wife left me; I have no money or friends, and I'm going to end it all right now." The passerby said, "Just give me ten minutes to talk to you. That's all I'm asking. Just ten minutes. Come sit with me in my car and let's talk." The disgruntled man stepped down off the railing and went and sat in the man's car. After ten minutes, they both jumped off the bridge.

1 Corinthians 15:33 Be not deceived: evil communications corrupt good manners.

Because He Lives

A little boy was sitting on the bank of pond fishing and singing softly, "Because He Lives." A man walked along and heard him singing and asked him what he was singing. The little fellow said, "I'm singing a song I learned in church called "Because He Lives." The man, being an atheist asked, "Who lives?" The boy said, "Jesus lives." The indignant man bellowed, "How do you know he lives? Can you see him, hear him, or touch him?" Just then the little guy got a bite on his hook and his rod started bobbing. He looked up at the man and said, "Salvation is like fishing. I can't see this fish. I can't hear this fish. I can't touch this fish, but I know he is there because I can feel him tugging on my line."

Romans 8:11 But if the Spirit of him that raised up Jesus from the dead dwell in you, he that raised up Christ from the dead shall also quicken your mortal bodies by his Spirit that dwelleth in you.

Becoming Royalty

Much media attention surrounded the wedding of Prince William and Catherine Middleton. The wedding took place on April 29, 2011 at Westminster Abby in London, England. What grabbed the world's attention was the fact that Catherine Middleton was a commoner, meaning she was not from a royal lineage. Kate walked into the church a commoner; she walked down the aisle to the altar as a commoner, and she stood before the priest who performed the wedding as a commoner. Yet when she made a vow to the Prince of Wales, she became royalty.

We were commoners living sinful lives in the world before we met our King. But the day we fell before him at the altar and made a vow, we became royalty.

1 Peter 2:9 But ye are a chosen generation, a royal priesthood, a holy nation, a peculiar people; that ye should shew forth the praises of him who hath called you out of darkness into his marvelous light.

Be Kind Anyway

A man was driving down the road and saw a squirrel that had been hit by a car writhing in pain in the middle of the street. He pulled over, got out of his car and went back to the squirrel. When he reached down to pick it up, the squirrel latched down on his hand and bit him with all its might. The man stopped to help the creature, but he ended up getting hurt.

Sometimes when you reach out to help someone who is in pain they will retaliate because it's their nature, but we must be kind anyway.

Luke 6:35 But love ye your enemies, and do good, and lend, hoping for nothing again; and your reward shall be great, and ye shall be the children of the Highest: for he is kind unto the unthankful and to the evil.

Be Still

Back before there were refrigerators, ice was kept in an icehouse. People would retrieve the ice in the winter from the rivers, and cut it into blocks, put the ice under sawdust, and seal the doors of the icehouse.

One day, the owner of an icehouse lost a very expensive watch and could not find it. He looked feverishly for the watch for many days, until one day his grandson came to him with the watch in his hand. He asked his grandson how he found the watch. The little boy said, "It was simple, Papa, I closed all of the doors, turned off the light and I got down with my ear in the sawdust and I listened carefully. When everything was still and quiet, I heard it ticking."

Sometimes it takes us being in the hospital, prison, sick bed, unemployment line, or divorce court, so we can here the ticking of God's voice.

Psalms 46:10 Be still, and know that I am God: I will be exalted among the heathen, I will be exalted in the earth.

Between a Rock and a Hard Place

In 2003 Aaron Ralston went hiking in the Blue John Canyon in Mid state Utah, which was his favorite pastime. It was a pleasant evening; the sun was brightly shining, and birds were chirping as a cool breeze kissed his face. He ascended a huge mountainous rock and his arm became caught behind 800 pounds of rock. Ralston did everything to dislodge himself but discovered that was impossible.

For five days and seven hours he remained trapped on the side of this mountain. He used all of the water and candy bars he had carried with him on this hiking expedition. He finally realized that if he didn't do something he was going to die of starvation or dehydration. Ralston remembered that he had a dull camping knife in his hiking bag. He took the knife and amputated his arm to extricate himself to save his life.

He wrote about this later in his autobiography and entitled it "Between a Rock and a Hard Place." It is a story of survival and the perseverance of the human spirit. It is a story of desperation. Between a rock and a hard place! Often in life we find ourselves in this very position between a rock and a hard place.

Exodus 14:1-3 Speak unto the children of Israel, that they turn and encamp before Pi-Hahiroth, between Migdol and the sea, over against Baal Zephon: before it shall ye encamp by the sea. For Pharaoh will say of the children of Israel, They are entangled in the land; the wilderness hath shut them in.

Biter or a Kicker

A farmer went to State Farm to buy some health insurance, and the agent asked him if he had had any previous accidents. The farmer said, "No, I've had no accidents. I was bitten by a rattle snake and a mule kicked me in the ribs which laid me up for a while, but I've had no accidents." The agent replied, "Sir, weren't those accidents?" The farmer replied, "No. They did it on purpose." We should be careful around rattle snakes and mules because it is natural for a snake to bite and a mule to kick. What is your natural attitude about life? Are you a biter or a kicker or do you just simply trust God and believe His Word when things go wrong in your life?

Proverbs 3:5-6 Trust in the Lord with all thine heart; and lean not unto thine own understanding. In all thy ways acknowledge him, and he shall direct thy paths.

Black Bart, Menacing Bully

From 1875 through 1883 Black Bart robbed 28 stagecoaches and accrued thousands of dollars from the Wells Fargo company. His modus operandi was to take the strongbox and rob the passengers on board as they traveled from place to place. Bart would take a canvas bag, cut four holes in the bag for his eyes, nose, and mouth. He also wore a long black overcoat with a bowler hat on his head and a shotgun in his hand.

History tells us that in spite of the fact that he robbed 28 stagecoaches successfully, he never fired a shot. His reputation traveled throughout the land, and people, including Wells Fargo, were afraid of this menacing figure. Wells Fargo offered a huge reward for his capture or death because he was costing them thousands of dollars each year. He never fired a shot, but he became one of America's greatest and most successful thieves by bullying people.

Here is the kicker--he never rode a horse. Why? He was gravely afraid of them. Like all bullies, Black Bart was a coward. The term bully is quite common in America today because we see it in virtually every aspect of American life. Many kids are bullied in school, in the classroom, on the playground, and on the school bus. Some kids are even bullied on social media. That's why you need to monitor your child's extracurricular activities. We read far too often in the headlines that some child has committed suicide because he has been bullied. Bullies are everywhere.

America was being bullied by an international group called ISIS. These people are arrogant militants who are bent on destroying anyone who befriends Israel. Steven Sotloff and Daniel Pearl were brutally murdered on camera by Islamic state bullies who wanted to send a message of their hatred for America.

Like all bullies, they have a fear and their fear is that our way of life may permeate their culture. I don't suppose there is a person here who does not know what it feels like to be intimidated by a bully. A bully intimidates, frightens, petrifies and causes much mental and emotional stress. Still, I want to share a course of action that believers can take when battling bullies. David faced a bully whose name was Goliath. He defeated him because he trusted God for protection. Don't let bullies intimidate you.

2 Timothy 1:7 For God hath not given us the spirit of fear; but of power, and of love, and of a sound mind.

Blessedness of Hot Water

A young girl comes home from college and is frustrated with school life. She walks into the kitchen and begins to talk to her grandmother who is laboring over the stove. She says to her grandmother, "I cannot take life anymore, I feel like giving up and quitting school."

The wise old grandma put three pots of water on the stove and turned up the heat until they began to boil. Then she put a potato in one pot, an egg in the other pot, and coffee beans in the third pot. Twenty minutes later she told the young girl to take the potato and egg and put them in a bowl, and pour the coffee in a cup. Then she said, "What do you see?" Young girl said, "I see potatoes, eggs, and coffee." Her grandmother said, "Look a little closer. Touch the potato and egg." Then she said to her, "Now taste the coffee. All three were placed in the same environment, but they all came out differently. The egg became hard, while the potato became soft, and the coffee changed its surrounding completely."

It is not always what happens to people, it is how they react to it. Some people become hardened by hardship, while others become soft. Like coffee, the believer does not become hard or soft because our environment shouldn't change us, but we should change our environment.

Romans 8:38-39 For I am persuaded, that neither death, nor life, nor angels, nor principalities, nor powers, nor things present, nor things to come, Nor height, nor depth, nor any other creature, shall be able to separate us from the love of God, which is in Christ Jesus our Lord.

Blessed With Overflow

When I was a little boy, my Dad always made me drink coffee in the morning. There was something about just standing there watching my Dad eat his food that I really enjoyed. He made it look so good. When Mom poured his coffee, she would fill the cup all the way to the top and some of it would spill over into the saucer. On many occasions Daddy would hand the saucer to me and I would sip from the overflow. When we stay in the presence of our Heavenly Father, He will always bless us with overflow.

Psalms 23:5 Thou preparest a table before me in the presence of mine enemies: thou anointest my head with oil; my cup runneth over.

Bow Down

Ancient merchants often had to cross deserts to take their merchandise to market, so they used camels. Camels, unlike horses, can travel long distances without drinking water. So, early in the morning the merchant would tell his animal to bow down and he would put a load on his back. As the camel walked during the morning, sometimes the load would shift, and around noon the master would tell the camel to bow down. The master would readjust the camel's load so that he could continue on his journey. When the day was done, the master would tell the camel to bow down and the master would take the load off the camel so that he could rest during the night.

If we are going to make it on our journey we must learn to bow before our master. Sometimes on our journey the master will put a load on us, not to break us but to strengthen us. Often, the load gets heavy, but he will not always take the load off. Sometimes he will readjust our load so we can bear it. The good news is the Lord knows exactly how much we can bear and he will take the load off us so we can rest if we will simply bow down.

Psalms 95:6 O come, let us worship and bow down: let us kneel before the Lord our maker.

Brain Power

To give you an idea of the function of the human brain you must imagine a wide receiver poised at the line of scrimmage. His brain must send messages to his legs when the signal is called by the quarterback to begin running down the field. Then he must turn, and his eyes must focus on the ball that has been released by the quarterback's hand and judge the height, the distance, and the proximity of where the ball will

16

fall. Then his brain must send commands through neurons down his spinal cord to his feet and legs to tell him to jump to receive the ball while extending his hands. Then the brain tells his fingers to close and grasp the ball, pull it securely to his side, while anticipating being hit by opposing players. His brain must do all of this, while controlling his heart rate, his breathing, blood pressure, and body temperature.

It's no wonder The United Negro College Fund slogan is, "A mind is a terrible thing to waste!" When the Bible speaks of the brain, it usually uses the term "heart." As the heart controls the human physicality of the human being, the brain controls emotion, will, thinking, and spirituality of humans. Therefore, the Bible says that we must not be duplicitous in our minds.

James 1:8 A double minded man is unstable in all of his ways.

Broken to Serve

A few months ago I carried some items to the King David landfill that were broken. I considered them useless. Among those items was a pivoting fan on a stand with a broken cord. I asked the attendant there which container I should put the fan into. He looked at it briefly and said, "Set it over here by my chair because there may be someone who can use it."

A week or so later, I went back to the same landfill and the guy had the fan right by his chair. It was pivoting from side to side blowing on him to keep the flies away. I learned something very interesting that day. Some things we throw away as useless are useful to others. It is trite but true. One man's trash is another man's treasure. Monkey Glue, Super Glue and Krazy Glue are great products for mending broken things, but there are some things glue won't fix.

As a pastor for over 26 years, I have seen a lot of brokenness precipitated by excruciating suffering. I've seen families torn apart by divorce, lives ravaged by disease. I've witnessed broken dreams, broken plans, and broken hearts. Through all of it, I have discovered the only thing that can mend a broken life is the blood of Jesus.

It's good to know God is in the recycling, the restoring, and renewing business. He never throws anything away. God is not a God of waste; He utilizes broken things. Some of us can testify that God used us in our brokenness. Many of us were told we would never amount to anything because of where we came from, what we didn't have, and what we didn't know but, God took us in our brokenness and He used us for his glory. As a matter of fact God uses nothing until he breaks it first. As Oswald Chambers said, "You can't drink grapes, they must be crushed."

2 Corinthians 12:6-7 For though I would desire to glory, I shall not be a fool for I will say the truth. Now I forbear, lest any man should think of me above that which he seeth me to be, or that he heareth of me. And lest I should be exalted above measure through the abundance of the revelations, there was given to me a thorn in the flesh, the messenger of Satan to buffet me, lest I should be exalted above measure.

Buzzard, Bat and the Bumblebee

You can catch a wild buzzard and put him in an open pen that's, let's say, 6 x 6, and he will die there. He cannot fly away. Why? A buzzard needs at least a 12- foot runway to take off. Take a bat, place him on the ground, and he will flop around there until he dies. Why? He can only achieve flight from an elevated position. He must launch out into the air. Take a bumblebee, put him in a tumbler, leave the top open, and that bee will never find his way out. He is so interested in trying to fly through the glass in front of him, he will never think to look up and find the way out. What is the point? All three of these, the buzzard, the bat, and the bumblebee all fail to notice the freedom that is right above them. As a result, they remain trapped in their prison.

Colossians 3:2 Set your affection on things above, not on things on the earth.

Can You Hear Me Now?

My dad's voice was the most recognizable sound in our house. When he spoke, everybody listened, including my mom. His voice was like E.F. Hutton: he got attention. Often, he would tell me, "Ronnie I want you to fill the hearth of the fireplace with wood while I am at work today." I later learned that he did that because he thought it would keep me out of trouble. He would also tell me, "While I'm at work today I want you to clear the weeds around the barn and gather vegetables from the garden for your Mom to cook." These were not suggestions they were commands.

Fathers have a right to do that, you know. After giving those commands he would conclude by asking, "Do you hear me?" He did not mean, "Do you hear me?" He meant, "Do you hear me!" Only an African-American boy from the country would understand the difference. If for whatever reason I did not obey my father, there would be dire consequences.

He would dislodge a long branch he kept over the door sill from an oak tree, and then apply the rod of correction to the seat of knowledge. I can still hear the sound of the switch being pulled from the top of that door. My dad believed in chastisement for disobedience. If I disobeyed my dad, he would issue corporate punishment.

Our heavenly Father will chastise us when we disobey Him, and we should chastise our children when they disobey us. The Bible says, "Whom the Lord loves he chastens," (Hebrews 12:6) so chastisement is evidence of love. The Bible goes on to say that if we don't chastise those we love, they are not ours but bastards.

Often God places His children in uncomfortable places because of our disobedience, and asks, "Can you hear me now?" This is what He did with the prophet Jonah.

Jonah 3:1, 2 And the word of the Lord came unto Jonah the second time, saying, Arise, go unto Nineveh, that great city, and preach unto it the preaching that I bid thee.

Check God's Credit History

The bottom line is God wants us to remember what He has done for us so that he can get credit. I learned when I bought my first house how important credit history is in buying any product. The three agencies in America that keep record of credit history are Experian, Equifax, and Transunion. These agencies monitor buying history to determine financial trustworthiness. If an individual applies for credit, these agencies determine whether or not that person can be trusted with a loan. If a person has defaulted on a past financial contract, it lessens the likelihood that he will get approval for a future loan.

I have checked out God's credit history and I have discovered that He has never defaulted on a contract. When he delivered Israel from dragging the clinking chains of slavery in Egypt, he gave them water out of the rock and bread from heaven. He scrambled the navigation system of birds and caused them to fly into the camp of Israel, so that they would have meat to eat. He altered the nature of ravens and turned them into butchers and bakers who fed the prophet Elijah down by the brook of Cherith. God's credit is impeccable.

Psalms 37:25 I have been young, and now am old; yet have I not seen the righteous forsaken, nor his seed begging bread.

Cherpie's Lost Song

Cherpie the parakeet sang all the time. He sang all day and all night. His owners had to put a canvas over his cage at night so they could get some sleep.

One day his owner decided to clean his cage with a vacuum cleaner. She removed the attachment from the end of the hose and stuck it in the cage. Not paying attention, she accidentally placed the nozzle too close and Cherpie got sucked into the bag. The bird owner gasped, turned off the vacuum, and opened the bag. There was Cherpie still alive, but severely dazed.

Since the bird was covered with dust and soot, she grabbed him and raced to the bathroom. She placed him under the faucet, and the cold water chilled Cherpie to the bone. Then, realizing that Cherpie was soaked and shivering, she did what any compassionate bird owner would do. She reached under the sink and grabbed her hair dryer and blasted him with hot air. The bird never knew what hit him.

When her husband came home, he noticed that Cherpie wasn't singing but said nothing. The next day, there still was not one note from Cherpie. Days went by, and all the bird did was sit in his cage and stare into blank space. Finally the woman's husband asked, "What's wrong with Cherpie?" "Well, honey, Cherpie doesn't sing anymore because he was sucked in, washed up and blown over." A lot of Christians are just like Cherpie. They have lost their praise because life has sucked them in, washed them up, and blown them over.

Psalms 137:1-3 By the rivers of Babylon, there we sat down, yea, we wept, when we remembered Zion. We hanged our harps upon the willows in the midst thereof. For there they that carried us away captive required of us a song; and they that wasted us required of us mirth, saying, Sing us one of the songs of Zion.

Children Of Value

The United States Treasury brings in hundreds of thousands of pounds of paper each day. In fact, it's the same paper we use in the bathroom, the same paper that's used to wrap the burgers at Burger King, the same paper we use to write notes, and clean toilets. But when they take the same paper and stamp the front and the back, it becomes money. Why? It's because it has been claimed as legal tender for the government.

Did you know that you don't own that dollar in your pocket or purse? It belongs to Uncle Sam. It's in circulation on behalf of Uncle Sam. We are valuable not because we are valuable but because we have a stamp of approval by God and we are in circulation to do His bidding.

We are adopted, appointed, accepted, and anointed. We are beloved, born again, and blessed. We are children, created in his image, and courageous. We are developed, different, and delivered. We are elect, edified, and encircled by angels. We are fathered by God, friends of the faith, and faithful. We are glad, gracious, glorified and gifted. We are holy, happy, and higher called. We are imperishable, informed, and blessed with increase. We are joyful, jewels, and justified. We are known of God, kings, and kinsmen. We are leaders, lights, and lamps. We are made in His image and overcomers. We are purified, pure, and precious. We are quickened by the Holy Ghost. We are refined, regal, and royal. We are sons, servants, seated in the heavenlies. We are His temple, taught by the Holy Ghost, and His tabernacle. We are unblemished, undefiled, and united. We are valuable, valiant, and His vessels. We are warriors and His workmanship. We have been x-rayed and the zenith of God's creation. It's simply great to be a child of God!

Psalms 139:14 I will praise thee; for I am fearfully and wonderfully made: marvelous are thy works; and that my soul knoweth right well.

Chosen

When I was a teenager, my friends and I often played basketball at Stockman Park in Greenwood. Believe it or not, I was not that good at playing basketball at that time. Often the best players would be the ones who played because the captains would choose the players they knew could help them win. David was better than most of the guys who came to play with us. One day, I was standing on the fence and David was choosing his team. He called my name. I could not believe that David chose me to play with him, but we won the game. The truth is David won most of the games because he was just that good. You see David didn't need me, but he saw me standing on the fence, and he knew I wanted to get in the game.

God through his foreknowledge chose us before the foundation of the world because He knew we would want to get in His game. He knew that our hearts would be fertile soil for His Word so He chose us for His team. He chose us not because we are so good but because He is so gracious.

Ephesians 1:4 According as he hath chosen us in him before the foundation of the world, that we should be holy and without blame before him in love:

Christian Luminaries

I bought some landscaping lights and installed them around my property, but they would not shine at night. I went back to Lowe's and complained to the service manager, thinking I had bought a dud pack of lights. He asked me how long I allowed them to stay in the sun, and I asked him why he was asking me that question. He responded, "These lights are solar powered and must be in the sunlight for at least eight hours before they will light up at night."

It struck me that this principle applies, not only to solar lights, but to believers as well. Before we can shine in a dark world, we must spend some time in His presence. He is the light of the world, and we only reflect the light that we absorb from Him.

Matthew 5:16 Let your lights so shine among men that they will see your good works and glorify your Father who is in heaven.

Clean Your Windows

Years ago, ladies in many neighborhoods would hang their laundry on a clothes line. One day, a young wife looked out her window and saw her neighbor's clothes on the line. She said to her husband, "Honey, come here and look at her dirty clothes, those whites are so dingy!" The young husband looked out the window, but said nothing.

The following week, while washing dishes, she looked from her window and saw her neighbor's clothes hanging and again, she said to her husband, "Maybe I need to go over there and give her some tips on how to wash clothes. She is probably using the wrong detergent." Still her husband remained silent. Every time her neighbor would hang her wash to dry, she would make the same disparaging comments.

The next week she went to her window and looked out, and to her surprise, her neighbor's clothes were perfectly clean and the whites were bright. She said to her husband, "Look, she's finally learned how to wash correctly. I wonder who taught her how to do it?" Her husband said, "No one dear, I got up early this morning and cleaned our windows."

Matthew 7:5 . . . First cast out the beam out of thine own eye; and then shalt thou see clearly to cast out the mote out of thy brother's eye.

Collecting on the Guarantee

A friend of mine bought a new car and was not satisfied with the exhaust system. He is old school, so he likes his car to have a dual exhaust system. He decided to take his new car to a muffler shop and have duals put on his Chrysler 300 so it would have a deep gurgling sound like a race car. When he took his car in for service at the dealership, he was disappointed to find they would not touch his car. He requested a meeting with the manager to discover why they refused to work on his car. The manager told him his car had been altered from its original state. Alterations were strictly forbidden by the warranty; therefore, the warranty was void. He followed by saying, "You can't collect on the guarantee if you don't follow the instructions." Many Christians are trying to hold God to His promise of his blessings, but they have voided the warranty by not following His instructions.

2 Chronicles 7:14 If my people, which are called by my name, shall humble themselves, and pray, and seek my face, and turn from their wicked ways; then will I hear from heaven, and will forgive their sin, and will heal their land.

Comebackability

I was sitting on my patio one day watching my kids and grandkids as they were swimming in the pool in our backyard. They were playing with a beach ball, and every time they rode it under the water, it would pop back up to the surface. I wondered why the ball would not stay under the water and it dawned on me the ball had something on the inside that would not let it stay down.

We have the Holy Ghost on the inside of us and He will not let us stay down. Though people have lied on us, hated on us, and counted us out, we always come back. We have comebackability. This is what the Resurrection of Jesus teaches us. No matter what they do to us on Friday, Sunday morning is just a few hours away, and we will come back.

1 Corinthians 15:16-18 For if the dead rise not, then is not Christ raised: And if Christ be not raised, your faith is vain; ye are yet in your sins. Then they also which are fallen asleep in Christ are perished. If in this life only we have hope in Christ, we are of all men most miserable.

Companion Who Understands

A man went to a dog pound to buy a dog. There were all kinds of dogs available, beagles, boxers, chows, and dachshunds. The man, being a dog lover, found it difficult to make up his mind which dog he wanted. So he asked the pound operator if there were any more dogs available. The operator said that there was one in the back that no one wanted, and he was scheduled to be put to sleep. The man asked to see the animal.

They walked to a back room and there was a three-legged dog that had lost one of its legs in an accident. The man said, "That's the one I want!" After the paper work was done and the man was about to walk out the door with his newly acquired friend, the pound operator asked, "Out of all these dogs we have available here, why in the world do you want a three-legged dog?" The man pulled up his pant leg and revealed a prosthetic and said, "I want a companion who understands."

Hebrews 4:15 For we have not an high priest which cannot be touched with the feeling of our infirmities; but was in all points tempted like as we are, yet without sin.

Complaining Father

A man had a habit of complaining about the food his wife placed before him at family meals before he gave the blessing. One day after his usual combination of complaint followed by prayer, his little girl asked, "Daddy, does God hear us when we pray?" "Why, of course," he replied. "He hears us every time we pray." She paused a moment, and then asked, "Does he hear everything we say the rest of the time?" "Yes, dear, every word," he replied, encouraged that he had inspired his daughter to be curious about spiritual matters. However, his pride quickly turned to humility when she asked, "Then which does God believe, our prayers or our complaints?"

Philippians 2:14-16 Do all things without murmurings and disputings: That ye may be blameless and harmless, the sons of God, without rebuke, in the midst of a crooked and perverse nation, among whom ye shine as lights in the world; Holding forth the word of life; that I may rejoice in the day of Christ, that I have not run in vain, neither laboured in vain.

Complaining Grandpas

Three senior citizens were golfing together, and two of them griped endlessly. "The fairways are too long," said one. "The hills are too high," said the other. "The bunkers are too deep," said the first again. Finally the third man said, "At least we're on the right side of the grass."

Psalms 118:24 This is the day which the Lord hath made; we will rejoice and be glad in it.

Complaining Monk

A monk joined a monastery and took a vow of silence. After the first year, his superior called him in and asked, "Do you have anything to say?" The monk replied, "Food bad." After another year the monk again had opportunity to voice his thoughts. He said, "Bed hard." When the third year went by he was called in before his superior again. When asked if he had anything to say, he responded, "I quit." His superior said, "It doesn't surprise me a bit. You've done nothing but complain ever since you got here."

Psalms 100:4 Enter into his gates with thanksgiving, and into his courts with praise: be thankful unto him, and bless his name.

Complaining Woman

A woman walks into Macy's complaint department with a candle holder in her hand and bellowed to the desk clerk, "This thing came yesterday by UPS that I didn't order, and I need to exchange it." The compliant, calm and reserved receptionist said, "I'm so sorry ma'am for your inconvenience, do you have your receipt?" "Yes!" shouted the woman, as she pulled out a piece of paper and handed it to the clerk. The nice attendant took the receipt and walked to the back and returned a few minutes later with a catalog. She then pointed to the item number which was the exact one on the candle and said, "This is the one you ordered and this number verifies it."

The belligerent woman pulled the catalog across the counter closer to her and said, "You're right, but this is the one I wanted." As she pointed to the candle holder beside the one she had in her hand. The attendant then said, "Well we have this one in the store. I'll call over to the claims department and you can walk right over and pick it up. They will have it waiting for you when you get there."

We often spend too much time at the complaint window when we ought to be at the claims department. Many of us don't realize that complaining is a sin.

Psalms 116:17 I will offer to thee the sacrifice of thanksgiving, and will call upon the name of the Lord.

Consequences of Choice

We are free to choose, but we are not free to choose the consequences of our choice. If I jump off the top of a 100-story building, that would be a bad choice. I was free to choose, but I am not free to change the consequences of that choice. There was a guy who jumped off the 100th floor of a building once and a drunk guy on the 80th floor saw him free falling past his window, and said, "Groovy man, how you doing?!" The guy who was falling said, "Alright, right now!" You see it's not the jump that's painful, it's that sudden stop. Some of us have chosen to disobey God's call to salvation and we're doing okay right now, but there will eventually be a sudden stop.

1 Kings 18:21 And Elijah came unto all the people, and said, How long halt ye between two opinions? If the Lord be God, follow him: but if Baal, then follow him. And the people answered him not a word.

Couldn't Have Made It Without You

A grandfather was walking with his grandson one day on a nature walk, and the little boy ran ahead of his grandad. In the distance, he could see a stream of water, and he knew his grandson could not cross over it. He turned and looked back at his granddad and said, "Papa, I can't go any further." The old man said to him, "Wait until I get there." Once he arrived at the stream, the old man picked up the boy and put him on his shoulder, and then carried him across the dyke. When they got to the other side, he put him down and the little boy looked back at him and said, "Papa I wouldn't have made it across if you had not helped me."

Psalms 124:2-4 If it had not been the Lord who was on our side, when men rose up against us: Then they had swallowed us up quick, when their wrath was kindled against us: Then the waters had overwhelmed us, the stream had gone over our soul:

Covering the Fallen

In January, 2007, Wesley Autrey witnessed a man having a seizure who then fell onto a New York subway track. Autrey saw the lights of an oncoming train, and left his two daughters, who were with him, to the charge of a woman standing nearby, and leaped on the tracks and covered the fallen man.

The train ran over Autrey and the fallen man, and he was so close to death that the grease from the bottom of the train was on his baseball cap when he came from under the belly of the train. He is called the Subway Superman because he covered a fallen man. I rejoice today I am covered by my Superman who covered my sins at Calvary.

Psalms 32:1 Blessed is he whose transgression is forgiven, whose sin is covered.

Cram for the Test

Two little boys were playing in the yard. One of their grandmothers was sitting on the porch in a rocking chair reading the Bible. The next day the same two little boys were playing in the yard, and grandma was still in on the porch reading the Bible. The third day, the grandmother was still on the porch rocking and reading her Bible.

One of the little boys looked at his friend and said, "Why is it that your grandma always sits on the porch reading the Bible?" His friend's response was, "I really don't know, but I do know that when I'm getting ready to be tested at school, I always cram for that test."

James 1:2-4 My brethren, count it all joy when ye fall into divers temptations; Knowing this, that the trying of your faith worketh patience. But let patience have her perfect work, that ye may be perfect and entire, wanting nothing.

Creation

Everything above the ground came out of the ground, and everything on the ground will eventually go back into the ground. Man cannot create nor can he destroy, he can only transform what came out of the ground into another form. Man can take iron ore and blast it in a furnace, smelt the impurities out of it, add carbon, and make iron and steel to make automobiles for transportation. Man can take particles of glass, mix it with fiber, and flatten it into a sheet, and make fiber glass to make boats for him to sail. Man can extract clay from the Earth, and mix it with water, place it in an oven, and make brick to build him a house to live in.

Man can take sand from the beach, mix it with cement, and make mortar to stabilize bricks in a wall. Man can take sulfur, charcoal, and potassium nitrate, mix it together and make gun powder to kill. Man can take crude oil, which is a mixture of hydrocarbons, and refine it to make gasoline to empower his machines. Man can take fire and wind, force it through his jet engines, and defy gravity to launch huge planes into the air to travel from one continent to another. But Man cannot create anything; he can only transform that which comes from the ground.

Genesis 1:1 In the beginning God created the heaven and the earth.

Cross Is a Plus Sign

A little boy was walking down the street crying when he was spotted by the police. The policeman walked up to the little lad and asked him why he was crying. The little fellow said, "I'm lost, and I don't know how to get home." The cop asked, "What is your address?" The boy said, "I don't know." The cop asked, "Well what is your dad's name?" The boy said, "Daddy." He then asked, "What is your mother's name?" The kid responded, "Mommy."

The cop thought for a moment, then he asked the boy if there was some kind of landmark close to his house. The boy said, "I live right next to a building with a plus sign on top of it." The cop knew he lived next to a church. He drove past several churches until he found the little boy's house. When the cop left the home of the boy, he began to think of how right the boy was. The Cross is a plus sign.

Being saved takes nothing from us it adds to our life. Jesus died giving. He gave his back to the Cross. He gave his hands to the nails. He gave his side to the spear. He gave his head to the thorns. He gave his life for our salvation. He gave his body to the grave. He stayed in the grave all night Friday, all day Saturday, all Saturday, but early Sunday morning, he got up taking the victory from the grave. He took the sting out of death. He took power from the devil. He took away our sins. He took away our shame. He took away hopelessness. He took away sorrow. Thank God for the Cross.

Colossians 2:13-15 And you, being dead in your sins and the uncircumcision of your flesh, hath he quickened together with him, having forgiven you all trespasses; Blotting out the handwriting of ordinances that was against us, which was contrary to us, and took it out of the way, nailing it to his cross; And having spoiled principalities and powers, he made a shew of them openly, triumphing over them in it.

Cross's Mission

Over two thousand years ago, a man hewed down a tree and laid it on the ground. Then he cut down another tree and laid it across the first tree. What he didn't realize was that he had created the mechanism by which Jesus would accomplish his mission.

That first tree was stuck in the Earth and pointed towards heaven. The second tree pointed from East to West. The first tree represented the restoring of the union between God and man and the second tree pictures the joining together of all mankind everywhere. The first tree eliminated all barriers between God and man, (We can come boldly to the Throne of Grace). The second tree symbolizes a complete brotherhood of men, red and yellow, black and white.

Ephesians 2:16 And that he might reconcile both unto God in one body by the cross, having slain the enmity thereby:

Dad Held My Hand

A little girl had a dentist appointment and she was really afraid. He father told her, "Darling you have to go to the dentist to see about your teeth." The little girl, with tears in her eyes, looked up at her dad and said, "I will go if you will go and hold my hand."

When the little girl got home, her mother asked her, "Did it hurt, and did you feel any pain?" She said, "Yes, it did, but as long as I knew that dad was holding my hand, I knew everything would be alright."

Hebrews 13:5 Let your conversation be without covetousness; and be content with such things as ye have: for he hath said, I will never leave thee, nor forsake thee.

Dads and Decisions

We've all heard the story of the soldier during the Civil War who couldn't make up his mind what side he would fight on. He couldn't decide if he wanted to wear gray for the south, or the blue for the north, so he bought a gray coat and some blue pants. He ended up being shot in the chest by the North and shot in the leg by the South.

The most important decision you will make today is to make your own decision because if you don't make a decision your decision is already made for you. God leaves all decisions concerning the family in the hands of the fathers. You see, in the natural, anything with two heads is a freak. The head of the Godhead is God the father, the head of the Church is Christ, and the head of the home is the father. God is a God of order. Just because something is different does not make it unequal.

A woman is different from a man, but that does not make her unequal to a man. If I cut an apple in half, I will have two different halves. They would be totally equal even though they are different. A woman is equal to a man, but different. How long is it going to take us to learn that? A man is not superior to a woman, and a woman is not inferior to a man. But a man is superior to a woman at being a man, and a woman is superior to a man at being a woman.

God has given man the responsibility of ruling the home, which means the final decision should be left in his hands. That doesn't mean that decisions aren't made together, it's just that the final decision is the father's. Paul says that the deacon, the godly man, should rule his house well. With responsibility comes accountability. Every father who has produced a family is ultimately responsible for that family to God. A father must give an account to God for what happens under his roof because God left him in charge.

It is incumbent, and it is mandatory that every father make a decision to serve the Lord. It begins with a decision.

Joshua 24: 15 And if it seem evil unto you to serve the Lord, choose you this day whom ye will serve; whether the gods which your fathers served that were on the other side of the flood, or the gods of the Amorites, in whose land ye dwell: but as for me and my house, we will serve the Lord.

Dance With My Father Again

A seven-year-old boy, his two sisters, and his brother are playing Monopoly in their small apartment in the Lower East Side of Manhattan. His mother hasn't had time to pull off her nurse's uniform she wears to work every day because she wants dinner on the table when her husband arrives home from his upholstering job. The smell of pork chops and mashed potatoes permeate the air which whets the appetite of the kids as they argue over whose turn is next.

Their father steps in with a great big smile on his face and all of the kids leap from their cherished game and rush toward him as he lifts the seven-year-old boy into the air. They all sit down to the table and enjoy the delicious meal their mom has prepared. One by one their dad listens attentively as each one of the kids recaps their day at school. After dinner their dad takes them to the small den and turns on the phonograph he bought the little boy for Christmas. They all dance around the little apartment. Everyone is laughing and enjoying each other as the music plays. The little boy wonders how his dad has so much energy after working all day, but they all continue dancing.

Someone reading this may be separated from the Heavenly Father, longing for the joy, peace and tranquility you once enjoyed. I have good news, you can get it back. In my childhood, we were taught that dancing is a sin. I can still hear the words that ring in my ear from the song an old deacon who sang, "Don't let him catch you on the dance floor."

As I grew, however; and learned more about God, I discovered that dancing is an expression of happiness, joy, and excitement. I also discovered that every culture from the dawn of time expressed themselves by dancing. From the Aborigine of Australia, to the cultured elite of Great Britain, all enjoy dancing. The people of the hills have the square dance, folk of the foothills have the achy breaky, the Baby Boomers have the electric slide, the Irish have the river dance, the Polish have their folk dance, the Native American have their Rain Dance, The Hispanic have their Mexican Hat dance, and Millennials have the Nay Nay and the Snake. But the church has the holy dance.

The Bible tells us to dance. It says praise the Lord with the dance. David danced before the Lord with all his might and Jesus included in this parable a reference to dancing to express joy and happiness. What makes dancing fulfilling is your partner. It's not necessarily the dance itself but who you're dancing with. Therefore, Jesus sets the parable of the returning prodigal on the backdrop of a festive of celebration where he dances with his father again.

Luke 15:22-25 But the father said to his servants, Bring forth the best robe, and put it on him; and put a ring on his hand, and shoes on his feet: And bring hither the fatted calf, and kill it; and let us eat, and be merry: For this my son was dead, and is alive again; he was lost, and is found. And they began to be merry. Now his elder son was in the field: and as he came and drew nigh to the house, he heard music and dancing.

Dance Until You Get Your Vision Back

In 1964 Cassius Clay (Mohammed Ali) fought Sonny Liston for the heavy weight boxing championship in Miami, Florida. Liston had a reputation for being a shrewd but under-handed fighter. Liston came out in the fourth round with some oil of wintergreen on his gloves and set Clay's eyes on fire.

When Clay returned to his corner, he complained to his trainer, Angelo Dundee, that he could not see Liston's punches coming because his eyes were burning. Dundee did an amazing thing. He told Clay, "Go back out there and dance until you get your vision back." That was exactly what Clay did. He bobbed and weaved and danced and avoided Liston the entire fifth round.

Finally in the sixth round he won when Liston refused to answer the bell. Sometimes saints must follow this method when the enemy attacks and blinds us from ultimate victory. Just dance until you get your vision back.

2 Samuel 6:14 And David danced before the Lord with all his might; and David was girded with a linen ephod.

Dangerous Bible

I was standing in line at the airport in Atlanta in front of a woman whose bag had been set aside for inspection. TSA made her stand in front of them as they went through the contents of her baggage. Before the agent opened the bag to start the search, she asked the lady if there was anything is in the bag that might hurt the agent as the bag was opened. The agent said, "Is there anything dangerous or sharp in this bag?" The lady said, "Yes." The agent hesitated and took a step backwards. Then the lady said with a smile, "My Bible is in there. It's sharp and dangerous to the devil's kingdom."

Hebrews 4:12 For the word of God is quick, and powerful, and sharper than any two-edged sword, piercing even to the dividing asunder of soul and spirit, and of the joints and marrow, and is a discerner of the thoughts and intents of the heart.

Dare To Be Different

The high jump in track and field is a sport dominated by the Russians for many years. Valeriy Brumel cleared the bar at seven feet three and three-quarter inches in 1960 and held the record for four consecutive years. Brumel used a technique called the belly roll in which the stomach was in a downward position as he rolled over the bar.

Dick Fosbury of Oregon State University found it difficult to develop and perfect this European technique because he could not coordinate his limbs in this fashion. Instead, of quitting the sport he loved, he developed what's called the Fosbury flop. With a rapacious dash, Fosbury would approach the bar with his shoulders, and with his belly up, he would roll his back over the bar. His technique was so effective that he shattered the world record. The sport of a high jumping has never been the same because Fosbury dared to be different.

There are cultural, societal, and academic pressures whose objective is to put us all in uniform, but God did not make us all alike. We are unique. We are distinct. We are all different by divine design. Different does not mean dysfunctional. Instead of despising our differences, we ought to embrace them. Our natural bodies are different biologically, emotionally and intellectually.

So it is in the body of Christ. The Bible teaches us that there is no fellowship between light and darkness, "Be ye not unequally yoked together with unbelievers: for what fellowship hath righteousness with unrighteousness? And what communion hath light with darkness?" 2 Corinthians 6:14. We are in the world but not of the world. "They are not of the world, even as I am not of the world." John17:16. We will be hated by the world, "If the world hate you, ye know that it hated me before it hated you." John 15:18. We are a "chosen people, a royal priesthood, and a holy nation." 1 Peter 2:9. Dare to be different.

2 Corinthians 6:17 Wherefore come out from among them, and be ye separate, saith the Lord, and touch not the unclean thing; and I will receive you.

Darkness Makes Us Shine

When hours of painstaking labor have gone into the creation of a diamond, the jeweler wants to show it off in the best possible way. That gem has been dug out of the ground, cut and polished to its finest hue. When it arrives at Kay's or Helzberg, that jeweler doesn't put it on a white background in the jewel case, he places it on a black felt cloth so that the beauty of the diamond shows forth.

God does this as well; he shows up when it is darkest in our lives. The woman with the issue of blood, Lazarus, the Israelites at the Red Sea all saw God move at the darkest day of their lives. Night can happen in your life. When you have more month than money, it's night. When you get laid off your job, it's night. When your son or daughter gets arrested, it's night. When your husband or wife wants a divorce, it's dark. When you're standing beside a freshly dug grave, it's night. When the doctor's report comes back positive, it's night. When pain is wrecking your body and the medicine is not helping, it's night. When friends turn away from you, it's night. But here's the good news.

Psalms 30:5 For his anger endureth but a moment; in his favour is life: weeping may endure for a night, but joy cometh in the morning.

D-Day At Calvary

On June 6, 1944, America and her allies landed on the beaches of Normandy, Germany. This is what historians call "D-day." This was a time that World War II broke the back of the Nazi regime of Hitler. The operation was called "Operation Bodyguard."

In order to invade Germany there was another operation put in place called "Operation Fortitude," which was a diversionary tactic. Operation Fortitude distracted the Germans by dropping dummy soldiers to the north of Normandy. Fake radio signals sent out misinformation to draw the Germans' attention away from Normandy. Fictitious generals were created using these signals to make the Nazis think that the attack would occur at Calais. All this was to cause distraction of the Nazis.

Over 2000 years ago another diversionary tactic occurred at Calvary. They thought that they were just killing a man, but they didn't realize that he was the God-Man. He walked like a man, talked like a man, ate like a man, slept like a man. They put a crown on him like a man: they beat him like a man; he died like a man; he was buried like a man, but early that Sunday he got up like God, and said "All power is in my hand!" The same power that caused him to breakthrough that tomb lives in us. It was a diversionary tactic by God the Father to defeat our enemy, the devil.

Matthew 28:18 And Jesus came and spake unto them, saying, All power is given unto me in heaven and in earth.

Deacon and the Drug Dealer

Bennie the Baptist went up to the microphone and prayed this prayer. "Lord I thank you that I have been in the church for forty years. I built this building with my bare hands because none of these people in front of me would lift a hand to help. Thank you, Lord that I was able to give more money in this church than anyone else because I gave more than a tenth of my income. Thank you Lord that I am one of the most dedicated members in this church. I don't smoke, I don't drink, and I sleep only with my wife. I don't lie all the time. I try to tell the truth even on my tax returns. When he finished, he slept through the sermon as always because he didn't like the pastor.

Meanwhile Pookie, the drug dealer who had just got out on bail, was sitting on the front seat listening attentively to the sermon. The pastor preached on grace that Sunday. When the preaching was over, Pookie bowed with tears rolling down his face and prayed this prayer. "Lord I'm the least person in this church to ask you anything, but please Lord have mercy on me. What I did was so bad that I can't even look up towards heaven. Lord I repent with everything in me for the sins that I have committed. Lord have mercy on me!"

Luke 18:14 I tell you, this man went down to his house justified rather than the other: for every one that exalteth himself shall be abased; and he that humbleth himself shall be exalted.

Death Is Not Final

Each week in America, paramedics arrive on the scene of an accident where the victim has crossed between life and death. No heartbeat. Breathing has stopped. All the vital signs of life are absent. Nevertheless, paramedics do not accept this death as final. They begin CPR and perhaps inject a drug that stimulates the heart. Sometimes the victim begins to cough and take a few breaths. The heart begins to beat, pulsing life through the body. Instead of sending a corpse to the morgue, the ambulance takes a patient to the hospital. Was the victim dead? We would have to answer, "Yes." If not for the care of the paramedics, the accident would have been followed by a funeral.

Revelation 3:2 Be watchful, and strengthen the things which remain, that are ready to die: for I have not found thy works perfect before God. Revelation 3:2

Death Means Waking Up In Your Own Room

A little girl couldn't sleep one night because the storm was raging outside. The lightening cracked the sky; the wind howled, and the thunder rolled like a thousand chariot wheels on heavens floor. She was afraid, so she got out of bed and went downstairs to her parents' bedroom and opened the door. Her father raised his head and said, "What's wrong darling?" She replied, "I can't sleep. I'm scared." Her father beckoned her to get in the bed with him and her mother. The little girl drifted off to sleep.

The next morning when she woke up, she discovered that she was back in her own room. In the middle of the night her dad had carried her back to her bed. That's what happens with us in the hour of death. When we leave this world, our father takes us to our own room.

John 14:1-3 Let not your heart be troubled: ye believe in God, believe also in me. In my Father's house are many mansions. If it were not so, I would have told you. I go to prepare a place for you. And if I go and prepare a place for you, I will come again, and receive you unto myself; that where I am, there ye may be also.

Define Your Own Destiny

Three men were placed on an island and told that they would have to remain there for the rest of their lives. They were also told that they would have the privilege of reading anything they wanted while they were there. The first man was asked what his choice of reading material was. He said, "I want the New York Times because I want to keep abreast of what's going on in the outside world." The second man was asked what he wanted to read. He responded, "I want Sports Illustrated because I want to keep up with what's happening with my favorite teams." The third man was asked what he wanted to read. He said, "I want Brown's Book on Boatbuilding because even though you put me on this island, I'm getting off."

Many of us have allowed others to determine our destiny by submitting to their assessment, assertions, and judgment of us. But if we are going to make a difference in this life, just as Michelle Obama said, "We cannot allow others to determine our destiny." We are to never submit to the will of others, only to God's.

I think to a large degree many believers in local churches are living lives beneath their privilege and enduring conquered lives because they are victims of identity theft. The forces of evil and the power of darkness have robbed many Christians of their identity. Many of us don't know who we are, whose we are, the plan that God has for our lives, or the purpose for our lives. In order for us to define our own destiny, we must recover our identity.

John 10:10 "The thief cometh not, but for to steal, and to kill, and to destroy; I am come that they might have life, and that they might have it more abundantly.

Devilish Blessings

There was an old Christian woman who had an evil atheist as a landlord. This infidel sought every opportunity to humiliate this old Christian. One night, as he was walking past her door, he overheard her praying. "Lord there's no food in my house and my check does not come until the third of the month. Lord you promised to supply my needs and not forsake me. Now Lord please send help. I have no one else to depend on but you."

The wicked old man seized the chance to make mockery of her Christian faith. He went down to the local BI-LO and bought two bags of grocery and used his pass key to enter her house while she was asleep. He waited until the next morning to see what would happen. That morning, the woman got up and saw the groceries on the dining room table and started shouting. "Praise the Lord, thank you Jesus!"

The landlord knocked on the door and she let him in, "What's all this yelling I hear?" he asked. She said, "Well Sir, last night before I went to bed I prayed to God for food and this morning when I arose there were groceries on my table!" The landlord smirked as he said, "You crazy old woman, I overheard you praying last night and went down to the grocery store and bought this food and put it on your table while you slept. If you want to thank someone, it ought to be me!" The old lady never stopped shouting, "Thank you Lord for this grocery even though you sent it by the devil."

Genesis 50:20 But as for you, ye thought evil against me; but God meant it unto good, to bring to pass, as it is this day, to save much people alive.

Devil's Tactics

I was watching National Geographic one night and I saw a clip about the wildebeest of Africa crossing a river. The alligators in the water waited patiently until all the strong and fit wildebeest had crossed because they knew instinctively that the weakest of the herd always straggle behind the rest. When the weakest that brought up the rear began to cross, the alligators pounced on them and destroyed them. Satan always attacks the weakest among us; therefore, every Christian should stay in the church. Those of us who live on the periphery are targets of the devil.

Deuteronomy 25:18 How he met thee by the way, and smote the hindmost of thee, even all that were feeble behind thee, when thou wast faint and weary, and he feared not God.

Devil Test

On the final exam, a seminary professor gave students two hours to complete their test. The assignment was a three- part question, which dealt with the material the class had covered in the past semester. In the first part, the students had to write two pages on the attributes of God. In in the second part, the students had to explain the works of the Holy Spirit in the life of the Believer. In the third section, students were asked to describe the origin and fall of the devil.

One young student started writing on the goodness, grace, and mercy of God. He remembered how the Lord had saved him from a miserable life of sin and kept writing. He remembered how God had comforted him through the Holy Spirit during the loss of his father and kept writing. His mind went back to when he had no money and thought he would have to drop out of school, but God provided his needs and kept writing. He looked up at the clock and there was only one minute left for the test and he had written nothing on the devil. So he put in parentheses at the bottom of his paper, "No time for the devil." When we concentrate on the goodness of God, we certainly will have no time for the devil.

Luke 4:8 And Jesus answered and said unto him, Get thee behind me, Satan: for it is written, Thou shalt worship the Lord thy God, and him only shalt thou serve.

Didn't Come To Read

Hank Aaron, the greatest hitter of all times, was standing at the plate as the Atlanta Braves played the New York Mets. Yogi Berra was catching that day and attempted to distract him. He told Aaron, "You're holding the bat upside down. Don't you know you supposed to be able to read the inscription on the bat? Can you read the bat brand Hank?" Just then the pitcher wound up, and Aaron connected with the ball and the ball went out into left field grandstand for a homerun.

Berra stood up with his cap in one hand and mask in the other as he watched the ball go through the air while Aaron jogged around the bases. As Aaron crossed home plate, he looked at Yogi Berra and said, "I did not come here to read, Yogi, I came to play baseball."

Nehemiah 4:1, 2 But it came to pass, that when Sanballat heard that we builded the wall, he was wroth, and took great indignation, and mocked the Jews. And he spake before his brethren and the army of Samaria, and said, What do these feeble Jews? Will they fortify themselves? Will they sacrifice? Will they make an end in a day? Will they revive the stones out of the heaps of the rubbish which are burned?

Dog Ate My Homework

A teacher gave an assignment to her class to complete worksheets and bring them back the very next day. All of the students took the worksheets home and completed them, but the teacher noticed that there was a little boy crying in the back of the class the next day. She walked over to the little boy and said, "Johnny what is wrong?" The little boy began to explain, "Teacher I completed my assignment, but when I turned my back, my dog came to the table and ripped apart the worksheet, so I don't have my assignment today."

The compassionate teacher went to her desk. She pulled out another worksheet, walked back to the back of the room, handed it to the little boy and said, "Johnny take this one home tonight and do better with this one." Ladies and gentlemen, aren't you glad that we serve a God who gives another chance? Every day you get out of your bed is another chance to do better. Every day you spend on the planet is another opportunity to do better. Every birthday is another chance to do better with your life. The Bible says that his mercies are fresh every morning. Enjoy your day, but do better with this one than you did yesterday.

Lamentations 3:22-23 It is of the Lord's mercies that we are not consumed because his compassions fail not. They are new every morning: great is thy faithfulness.

Don't Believe Fake News

Joshua and Caleb and all the children under the age of twenty were the only ones allowed to enter into the Promised Land of Canaan. The rest were assigned to encircle the wilderness until they died. Why, you may ask? It was because they chose to believe fake news. Joshua and Caleb chose to listen to the good news. What about you?

I have some good news and some bad news. The bad news is they arrested Jesus in the Garden of Gethsemane one Thursday night. The bad news is they beat him with 39 lashes with a whip of a cat of nine tails. The bad news is they placed a crown on his head and mocked him, calling him the King of the Jews. The bad news is that his trusted disciples abandoned him and ran like scared rabbits. The bad news is they crucified him that Friday evening. The bad news is they buried him in a borrowed tomb. The bad news is he stayed there all night Friday night. The bad news is he stayed there all day Saturday. The bad news is he stayed in the grave all Saturday night. But I have some good news. He got up!

The good news is he got up with all power in his hands. The good news is he took the sting out of death and won victory from the grave. The good news is that the same power that raised Jesus from the grave lives in you! The good news is because he got up and gave us his power, death can't kill us, the grave can't hold us, no demon can defeat us, and the devil can't control us. Ain't that good news?

Numbers 13:30-33 And Caleb stilled the people before Moses, and said, Let us go up at once, and possess it; for we are well able to overcome it. But the men that went up with him said, We be not able to go up against the people; for they are stronger than we. And they brought up an evil report of the land which they had searched unto the children of Israel, saying, The land, through which we have gone to search it, is a land that eateth up the inhabitants thereof; and all the people that we saw in it are men of a great stature. And there we saw the giants, the sons of Anak, which come of the giants: and we were in our own sight as grasshoppers, and so we were in their sight.

Don't Call the Police; Call Jesus

Dr. B.R. Daniels, who has conducted revivals at my church, said that he preached for a church in Chicago. The church was located in the red light district, and one night the cops were on the prowl. He and the pastor were back in the pastor's study when an usher ran into the office and said, "There is a prostitute in the vestibule." The pastor said to the usher, "Call the police!" Daniels said that he told the pastor, "We should call the police when a crime is committed, but we should call the Lord when sin is committed."

Romans 10:13 For whosoever shall call upon the name of the Lord shall be saved.

Don't Give Up On God

My dad became blind because of glaucoma before he died. One of my fondest memories of him was when he looked at me across the dinner table and said, "Ronnie, tell the church don't give up on God." He continued by saying that my mother, who suffers with diabetes, had a diabetic attack a few days earlier. She drifted in and out of consciousness and was delirious because of the drop in her sugar levels.

Dad said that he picked up the phone and attempted to dial for help, but because of his blindness he could not see the keys on the phone. He tried for approximately an hour, dialing number after number, but had no success with reaching anyone.

The devil began to talk to him and told him, God doesn't see you. God doesn't know you, and God doesn't care about you. With tears rolling down his cheek he said that the Holy Spirit began to speak and said try one more time. He picked up the phone and dialed seven numbers. My nephew Shae questioned, "Is everything alright granddaddy." In a matter of minutes the EMS responders were at my parents' house and took my mother to the hospital. Dad said tell the church don't give up on God.

What are the odds of a blind man dialing seven numbers and being successful in reaching someone he knows? I'm not a mathematician, but I think it's pretty slim. That is unless God is involved. Don't give up on God.

Matthew 6:26 Behold the fowls of the air. For they sow not, neither do they reap, nor gather into barns; yet your heavenly Father feedeth them. Are ye not much better than they?

Don't Let Him Catch You With Your Work Undone

In the summer months my father gave me chores to do around the house. He told me to cut wood and to work around the barn while he was at work during the day. But I remember once that I went fishing with my cousin and we stayed all day. Late in the evening I looked up at the sun and realized the day had passed. I rushed home knowing it was impossible to get everything done before dad came home. Usually, if I had done my assignments as he had told me, I would run into him, grab his lunch box, and hug him, but when he came home that day, I ran and hid from him.

What a thought, trying to hide from someone you can't escape. Many will run in the Great Day of the Lord and say to the mountains, "Hide us from the face of Him who sits on the Throne." Don't let The Lord catch you with your work undone!

1 Thessalonians 5:2 For yourselves know perfectly that the day of the Lord so cometh as a thief in the night.

Don't Throw Grandma Or Pookie Under The Bus

Some churches direct their ministry towards millennials and throw grandma and granddad under the bus. All their programs are for young folk. Then there are other churches that place all their emphasis on the seniors and have no concern whatsoever for the youth. But both these churches are overlooking God's plan for his church. God wants us to minister to all ages.

But how do we do it? How do we reach young people who say, "I like Kirk Franklin," and older people who say, "I hate that kind of music? I like hymns." How do we bridge the generation gap between the old and young? Young people are turned off by hooping and older people think you have not preached unless you hoop. It's actually pretty simple. Preach the truth; it never goes out of style.

Mark 13:31 Heaven and earth shall pass away: but my words shall not pass away.

Don't Wake Dad

A man who had been saved from a life of sin became a street preacher telling the good news of Jesus. One day, he was holding a tent meeting and giving his testimony of what the Lord had done for him. When he finished preaching, a man walked up to him and said, "Mister, what you're saying makes no sense. All this talk about Jesus and him saving you sounds stupid to me. You must be dreaming."

While the man was talking, a little girl walked up behind him and tugged his coat tail. She said to him, "Sir, my dad used to beat my mama. He would come home drunk, and we had no food to eat. My mom used to cry all day long. But now we have food to eat, my mom is always smiling, and there is happiness in our home. If my dad is dreaming please don't wake him up."

2 Corinthians 5:17 Therefore if any man be in Christ, he is a new creature: old things are passed away; behold, all things are become new.

Door Knob Is On the Inside

Jesus said, "I am the door to the sheep fold that the sheep must enter." He stands in front of the door to protect the sheep from thieves and robbers. There is another door: it's the door to your heart. Holman Hunt painted a picture of Jesus knocking at a door. The original piece hangs in St. Paul's Cathedral in London. His inspiration for this painting is Revelation 3:20. Some saw him painting this picture and said, "Mr. Hunt you made a mistake, there's no door knob on the door in the painting." To which he responded, "I've made no such error. There is a handle, but it is on the inside." Jesus is whispering to someone right now saying, "Open up and let me come in."

Revelation 3:20 Behold, I stand at the door, and knock: if any man hear my voice, and open the door, I will come in to him, and will sup with him, and he with me.

Door of the Ark

I'm reminded of the Old Testament story of Noah. The Bible says that the wickedness of mankind had spread across the Earth and God had determined that He would destroy all life by a flood. He called

Noah and gave him a blueprint of a boat that would be used to save him and his family. Noah obeyed God and built an ark according to God's specifications.

God told Noah to put one door in the side of the ship and one window up top. This huge sailing vessel had only one window and one door. Then God commanded Noah to take two of every species of animal into the ark along with his family. Noah obeyed.

Then there is a strange line in Genesis 7:16, "And they that went in, went in male and female of all flesh, as God had commanded him and the Lord shut him in." God shut the door behind them and sealed it so that no one else could get in. The same door that let some in shuts others out. The door is available to you today but one day that same door will shut you out. Come in the door today because tomorrow just might be too late.

Matthew 7:23 And then will I profess unto them, I never knew you: depart from me, ye that work iniquity.

Double Coverage On the Threat

I was watching the NBA playoffs between the Golden State Warriors and the Cleveland Cavaliers. During the game I noticed that Steve Kerr, who is the coach for Golden State, put double coverage on LeBron James. Each time James touched the ball, two of the Warriors would leave whoever they were playing and guard him. Kerr did that because James was the greatest threat on the Cavalier's team. Likewise, when you are a threat to the devil's kingdom he will put double coverage on you.

We must ask ourselves as Christians whether we are worthy of double coverage. If we are never attacked by Satan, then that may mean we pose no threat to his team. If you never meet the devil on the road that you are traveling, this could mean that you and the devil are traveling in the same direction.

1 Corinthians 16:9 For a great door and effectual is opened unto me, and there are many adversaries.

Do You Want To Go To Heaven?

One Sunday morning a preacher asked, "How many of you here today want to go to heaven?" Every hand in the church went up except one guy sitting in the corner of the church. The pastor thought that perhaps this guy didn't hear him, so he asked again, "How many of you in this church want to go to heaven?" The old man still sat placid in his seat. The preacher decided he would confront the man, so he asked him, "Sir, I just asked everyone here today if they wanted to go to heaven and every hand in this church was raised but yours. Don't you want to go to heaven?" The guy said, "Yes I do, when I die. I thought you were trying to get a load up right now. When I go, I want to be on the last bus on the back seat."

Where is heaven? There are three heavens as far as I can tell. If you would walk out and look up on a clear day, you would be looking into the first heaven. It is where the clouds float, and the birds fly. I fly quite a bit, and I often purchase a window seat because I want to look down from Heaven to see the Earth. It's a beautiful sight to see immaculately arranged squares of greenery from 30,000 feet.

The second heaven can be seen when the sun goes down. On a clear night, you can see the handiwork of God. Every parent should take their children out at night to view the heavens. They should show them the Big Dipper, the North Star, the Little Dipper, Alpha Centauri, the Loads Star, and dancing constellations, which are billions of light years from Earth. They should be careful to show them the twinkling stars, sparkling like diamonds on black velvet, the prancing meteors that trace the sky traveling at a million miles an hour, and the great Milky Way, glistening with an illuminate hue. They all testify that our God is the supreme architect of the universe.

But there is another heaven called the Third Heaven. The Apostle Paul spoke of it in 2 Corinthians 12: 2, "I knew a man in Christ above fourteen years ago, whether in the body, I cannot tell; or whether out of the body, I cannot tell: God knoweth. such a one caught up to the third heaven." There have been only three men who were privileged to see the third Heaven and lived to tell us about it--Paul, Isaiah, and the Apostle John. Neither of them could describe what saw in terms that the human being could really understand.

Let me recapitulate. The first heaven is where the birds fly, the clouds float, and planes fly. The second heaven is where the stars are and where the moon and sun are positioned. The Third Heaven is where God is. The first heaven you can see by day, the second heaven can be seen at night, but the Third Heaven can only be seen by faith. Where is heaven? It's up. How do I know? The last time Jesus was seen he was going upward. He said I'm going to my Father to prepare a place for you that where I am there you may be also. So, Heaven is up there somewhere because when Jesus returns we all will have to look up to see him.

Revelation 21:1-3 And I saw a new heaven and a new earth: for the first heaven and the first earth were passed away; and there was no more sea. And I John saw the holy city, New Jerusalem, coming down from God out of heaven, prepared as a bride adorned for her husband. And I heard a great voice out of heaven saying, Behold, the tabernacle of God is with men, and he will dwell with them, and they shall be his people, and God himself shall be with them, and be their God.

Dream Big

It started like so many evenings. Mom and Dad were at home and Jimmy was playing after dinner. Mom and Dad were absorbed with jobs and didn't notice the time. It was a full moon and some of the light seeped through the windows. Then Mom glanced at the clock. "Jimmy, it's time to go to bed. Go up now and I'll come and settle you later."

Nine-year-old Jimmy went straight upstairs to his room. An hour or so later his mother came up to check if all was well, and to her astonishment found her son was staring quietly out of his window at the moonlit scenery. "What are you doing, Jimmy?" "I'm looking at the moon, Mommy." "Well, it's time to go to bed now." As that reluctant boy settled down, he said, "Mommy, you know one day I'm going to walk on the moon."

Who could have known the boy in whom the dream was planted that night would survive a near fatal motorbike crash, which broke almost every bone in his body, and would bring to fruition this dream 32 years later. When James Irwin stepped on the moon's surface, He was just one of the 12 representatives of the human race to have done so? When James Irwin set foot on the moon, his words back to Houston were,

Psalms 121:1 I will lift up my eyes to the hills from whence cometh my help, my help come from the Lord which made heaven and Earth.

Dressed for a Dead Church

A homeless man showed up in a high church one Sunday morning. His clothes were ragged and tagged; he needed a shave; his hair needed to be combed, but he felt the need to go to church. Everyone in this church was well-dressed, but they were distant and cold. The pastor stood up and preached a long sermon, and while preaching, he kept watching this homeless man. When the choir began to sing, they too, were cold, and lifeless, and they kept watching this man. At the end of the service the pastor came up to the man and said to him, "I want you to pray and ask God how you should come to church. Next Sunday you should come dressed appropriately."

The homeless man showed up the next Sunday with the same ragged clothes and in the same condition. The pastor asked him, "Did you ask God how you should come to church to meet him?" The homeless man said, "I did, but God told me that he has never been here."

Revelation 3:1 And unto the angel of the church in Sardis write; These things saith he that hath the seven Spirits of God, and the seven stars; I know thy works, that thou hast a name that thou livest, and art dead.

Drinking Deacon

An old deacon was spotted coming out of the liquor store by another deacon. He decided to follow him to see what he was going to do with it. The first guy knelt down in an alley and turned up the bottle. His friend said to him, "You know you shouldn't do that. You know that the Lord sees you." The first deacon said, "Yes, I know, but the Lord ain't a big blabbermouth like a lot of people I know."

Galatians 6:1 Brethren, if a man be overtaken in a fault, ye which are spiritual, restore such a one in the spirit of meekness; considering thyself, lest thou also be tempted.

End of Trouble

A pastor was performing a wedding ceremony and at the end of the ceremony he said, "You are at the end of your troubles." One year later the young man came to the pastor and said to him, "I thought you said that I was at the end of my troubles. This year has been the worst year of my life." The pastor responded, "But I didn't say which end."

Job 14:1 Man that is born of a woman is of few days and full of trouble.

Enjoy the Ride

I checked into a hotel in Raleigh, NC. After I registered, I stepped onto the elevator to go up to my room which was located on the 19th floor. The doors shut on the elevator and I was standing there with my bags in my hand. The Holy Spirit spoke to me and asked, "What are you doing?" I replied, "I'm going up to my room." Then the Lord said, "You are carrying unnecessary weight. Put those bags down and let the elevator do the work for you." Then He said this, "You're going to make it to your destination because the elevator has already being programmed to your floor. Just enjoy the ride."

God is taking us to the next level of living, but many of us are frustrated because we are carrying unnecessary baggage. Put down those bags and enjoy the ride.

Hebrews 12:1: Wherefore seeing we also are compassed about with so great a cloud of witnesses, let us lay aside every weight, and the sin which doth so easily beset us, and let us run with patience the race that is set before us.

Examine God's Work History

Years ago I filled out an application for work at Wickes Builders Supply. The loading manager interviewed me for the job. When I sat down in his office, he asked me several personal questions like, "How old are you, are you married, do you have kids, where do you live?" After I answered all of his questions, he slid back in his chair and began looking over my application. He saw that I had worked previously at Worthington Tile Company, and he saw that I had worked at Greenwood Mills. He also saw that I had worked at Abney Mills. He saw my past work record and then he said something I will never forget. He said, "Well, I see that you will work because you have a record that you did work in the past."

When faced with a dilemma we should examine God's past work record, and we will be encouraged about anything that will come up in the future. What God has done is a good indication of what God will do.

Psalms 20:7 Some trust in chariots, and some in horses: but we will remember the name of the Lord our God.

Excessive Celebration

A few years ago the Dallas Cowboys were playing the New York Giants in New York. It was a close game, and New York was leading up until the last quarter. With just a few seconds on the clock, Tony Romo connected with Jason Witten in the end zone. Witten caught the ball, spiked it, and began to dance in the end zone. To the crowds amazement a referee threw a flag, and everybody with baited breath wondered why the flag was thrown. The referee clicked the little device on his side, and said, "Excessive celebration!" penalty to be enforced at kick off.

There will be people in the church who throw a flag on you for excessive celebration. But they don't know what you had to get through to get to the "in zone." There should be more Christians who get flagged for excessive celebration.

Psalms 149:3 Let them praise his name in the dance: let them sing praises unto him with the timbrel and harp.

Explain That

How do you explain the four seasons that come each year in sequential order? Spring, Summer, Fall and Winter? How do you explain a black cow eating green grass giving off white milk that churns yellow butter?

Explain this: A farmer puts a brown watermelon seed in the black earth. That seed germinates and turns white. That brown seed was put in the black earth and turns white. In three days, that white shoot turns green, and begins to run along the ground. That which was brown, placed in something black, comes up white, and then turns green. In a week, yellow flowers appear on the green vine. In a few weeks, a striped melon appears on that green vine with the red in it. That which was brown, placed in something black, turns white, and then turns green with yellow flowers, that turns into a striped melon with red on the inside, with the same brown seed that was placed in the ground, explain that!

Job 37:15-17 Dost thou know when God disposed them, and caused the light of his cloud to shine? Dost thou know the balancings of the clouds, the wondrous works of him which is perfect in knowledge? How thy garments are warm, when he quieteth the earth by the south wind?

Faith and Folk

Some people we are mad with right now have said something to us, but we forgot that the devil uses people closest to us in order get to us. The devil wants to destroy our faith and he uses those we love to neutralize our faith. He will use our spouses, children, and co-workers to get to us.

Ephesians 6:12 For we wrestle not against flesh and blood, but against principalities, against powers, against the rulers of the darkness of this world, against spiritual wickedness in high places.

Faithless Church

A club owner wanted to open up a business right next door to a church. When the members of the church heard about the club owner's plans, they began to pray that God would intervene and prevent the club from being opened. One night, lightning struck the club and burned it to the ground. When the club owner saw the ashes, he filed a lawsuit against the church and took them to court. The church filed a countersuit claiming they were not responsible.

When the judge on the bench read the case, he announced to the court room, "One thing I know is that the club owner believes in prayer and these Christians don't."

Mark 11:24 Therefore I say unto you, what things soever ye desire, when ye pray, believe that ye receive them, and ye shall have them.

Faith under Pressure

Our lives are much like popcorn. Many people enjoy this wonderful snack. Do you realize that this snack starts as a hard kernel of corn, but when it is subjected to the heat and put under pressure, it produces a great snack? It has to go through the heat and pressure before it explodes into this great snack called popcorn.

In a similar way, there will be times when we all face the fiery furnace, the fiery trial that Peter refers to. There will be times when we face circumstances that put our faith to the test, but in the end, they can produce an unshakeable trust in God and bring glory to a God who can do anything but fail.

1 Peter 4:12 Beloved, think it not strange concerning the fiery trial which is to try you, as though some strange thing happened unto you.

Fearful Farmer

An old farmer falls on hard times and he is at the verge of losing everything he has. His tractor payment is due; his farm note is due, and the house payment is due. He resolves to rob a bank knowing that he knows nothing about bank robbing.

He finally gets up enough nerve after riding around the bank several times. He places the gun in his pocket and walks up to the counter. When he stands in front of the counter, he slides the gun across the counter, points to the bag and the lady and says, "Put the money in the gun. This is a mess up." Fear can cause us to make fools out of ourselves.

Job 3:25 For the thing which I greatly feared is come upon me, and that which I was afraid of is come unto me.

Fear Monger

The devil is a fear monger. He has mastered the use of fear to stultify God's people. Most of the things we worry about never actually happen.

When I was a boy, the media was so sure that we were headed to nuclear war, so we learned in elementary school how to crouch under our desks, just in case. (Like that would do any good). Remember the swine flu? How about the bird flu? Y2K bug? Mad cow disease? The ozone has depleted so much that the world population will be cut in half in a few years, according to certain media outlets. All this frenzy is strategically designed by the enemy to keep us worried and distrustful of God's Word.

Yes, this world is headed to destruction, but God is still in the driver's seat, and He has made us some promises that will never fail. There are two reports for us today--God's report and the devil's report. The question is whose report will you believe? That's where the proverbial rubber of this text hits the road.

1 Peter 5:8 Be sober, be vigilant; because your adversary the devil, as a roaring lion, walketh about, seeking whom he may devour:

Finding Time for God

When we find time for Facebook, Twitter, Instagram, and Snapchat, but no time for prayer and Bible study, we give nothing.

When we work all week on our job but complain that we are too tired on Sunday to come to Sunday school, church service, and Bible study, we give nothing.

When we eat three meals a day that God has provided and find no time to fast, we give God nothing.

When we buy Nino Cerruti suits, Armani ties, Red Bottom shoes, Michael Kors purses but give only $10 in the offering, we have nothing.

When we find time to go to the movies to see "Black Panther," and sports arenas to watch our favorite teams and won't visit the sick and shut in members, we are giving God nothing.

When we are on time every day for work, but walk in church half late with a slow braggadocios swagger, we give God nothing.

When we have perfect attendance at work, but absenteeism at church, we give God nothing.

Nothing plus nothing equals nothing, nothing divided by nothing is nothing, nothing times nothing comes to nothing, and nothing from nothing leaves nothing, that's the reason why some of us have nothing.

Ask yourself this question, in what way am I giving to God?

Do you give God your time?

Do you give God your treasure?

Do you give God your talents?

Do you give God your best?

Do you give in a way that costs you personally?

Do you give him a portion of your resources?

Have you given him your family?

Are you giving God your seconds or your left overs?

Do you give to God because it is expected of you?

Do you give to God out of habit?

Do you do it because the offering is part of the service and you think people will notice if you don't give?

Do you give in a way that is rote or meaningless to you?

Do you give out of a heart of humility and gratitude to God?

Do you give out of a sincere desire to please him and to align yourself with his will?

Do you give out of a desire to personally shoulder the responsibility that goes with being a disciple of Jesus?

Psalms 116:12 What shall I render unto the Lord for all his benefits toward me?

Finish the Race

The Olympic Games were held in Mexico in 1968. The marathon was the final event on the program. The Olympic stadium was packed and there was excitement as the first athlete, an Ethiopian runner, entered the stadium. The crowd erupted as he crossed the finish line.

Way back in the field is another runner, John Stephen Akwhari of Tanzania. He has been eclipsed by the other runners. After 30 kilometers, his head is throbbing, his muscles are aching and he falls to the ground. He has serious leg injuries and officials want him to retire, but he refuses. With his knee bandaged, Akwhari picks himself up and hobbles the remaining 12 kilometers to the finish line.

An hour after the winner has finished, Akwhari enters the stadium on the last leg of the race. All but a few thousand have gone home. Akwhari moves around the track at a painstakingly slow pace until finally he collapses over the finish line. It is one of the most heroic efforts of Olympic history. Afterward, asked by a reporter why he had not dropped out, Akwhari says, "My country did not send me to start the race. They sent me to finish." Our reward is not at the start of the race, but after we finish.

2 Timothy 4: 6- 7 For I am now ready to be offered, and the time of my departure is at hand. I have fought a good fight. I have finished my course. I have kept the faith.

First Class Granny

An old mother received a plane ticket from her son to come visit him in Philadelphia for the Christmas holidays. She had never flown before so she was unfamiliar with the boarding procedure of the plane. When she entered the plane there were people who stared at her because of her shabby dress and the old purse she was carrying.

Not knowing any better, she sat down in the first available seat which was a First Class seat. One of the smug passengers looked at her and said, "You're in the wrong seat; you belong in coach." The mother responded, "My seat may be in coach, but I'm First Class."

Revelation 1:6 And hath made us kings and priests unto God and his Father; to Him be glory and dominion forever and ever. Amen.

Focused On Purpose, Not On Crowds

When we look at sit-coms and hear the laughing, we automatically assume that the laughter we hear is from an audience and we laugh also. It doesn't matter that the lame joke we just heard is not funny, but we laugh because we hear the laugh track that has been strategically placed there for the desired response. I don't know what your favorite sitcom is, but the laughter you hear is taped to give a sound effect to make you laugh. Sometimes you hear this, "This show was filmed before a live audience." They want to make sure you know that the laughs are for real!

We identify with crowds. If someone got up and ran out of church, you wouldn't get too upset, but if several got up and ran, I guarantee you would be behind them. It's just a spontaneous response. We associate with crowds. You wouldn't hang around with anyone you couldn't identify with, would you?

In 1992 there was rioting in LA because the policemen who mercilessly beat Rodney King were acquitted. King and been stopped by cops in LA and secretly recorded on tape by a pedestrian who released the film to the media. Widespread looting, assault, arson, and killings occurred during the riots, and estimates of property damage were over $1 billion. In total, 63 people were killed during the riots, 2,383 people were injured, and more than 12,000 were arrested after the police were acquitted.

Here's the thing. Some of the people who participated in the riots had no previous record. They were simply inspired by the crowds. March Madness and Mardi Gras are also examples of our innate tendency to follow the crowd. Jesus was never moved by crowds. The Bible says the he knew what was in the heart of men. He teaches us to let nothing or anyone sway us from our purpose and assignment. Jesus stayed focused on his purpose not on crowds. May we follow His example.

John 6:15 When Jesus therefore perceived that they would come and take him by force to make him a king, he departed again into a mountain himself alone.

Following Daddy

One spring morning I followed my dad to the garden to pick string beans. Early that day there had been a morning shower, and I noticed that he was carefully placing his feet in certain areas as he walked through the garden. He was avoiding getting his feet muddy. When I saw his tracks I began to walk in his footsteps to keep from getting mud on my feet. He turned around and said, "Ronnie what are you doing?" I said to him, "Daddy I am walking in your footsteps because if you don't get mud on your feet I won't get any on mine."

1 Corinthians 11:1 Be ye followers of me, even as I also am of Christ.

Forgotten Sins

A pastor was counseling a young man who had committed a public sin and the whole community was talking about it. The old minister was trying to show the young guy how God forgives and he used this verse as encouragement. "Behold, for peace I had great bitterness: but thou hast in love to my soul delivered it from the pit of corruption: for thou hast cast all my sins behind thy back." Isaiah 39:17 But the young man said, "Well pastor if the Lord has put all my sins behind Him that means when he turns around, won't He see my sins?" The preacher replied, "No, it doesn't. Notice the verse did not say that God has placed our sins behind Him, but He has put them behind His back. That means when God turns around, our sins remain behind Him."

Micah 7:19 He will turn again, he will have compassion upon us; he will subdue our iniquities; and thou wilt cast all their sins into the depths of the sea.

Foretaste Of Glory

As a little boy, I thought nobody could cook cakes like my mother. I would watch her as she made her famous pound cake, with tiptoe anticipation. I would wait until she finished pouring the cake batter into the pan. She would then look down at me and hand me the pan and the spoon and allow me to lick the spoon. What Mom was doing was giving me a foretaste of the cake. It was not the finished product, but just a foretaste for what was to come.

When God answers our prayers that is just the foretaste of what is to come for us in glory. When he allows us to feel his presence and peace in the midst of the storm, that's a foretaste. The beloved hymn says, "Blessed assurance, Jesus is mine. Oh, what a foretaste of glory divine."

Hebrews 6:4-5 For it is impossible for those who were once enlightened, and have tasted of the heavenly gift and were made partakers of the Holy Ghost, And have tasted the good word of God, and the powers of the world to come.

Fruit Bearing Brothers

When two little brothers were mischievous, they were banished to their bedroom. What their mother and father didn't know was that they would open the window to their room and climb down a fruit tree right next to the house and go play in their neighbor's yard. It was an ingenious plan, they had a perfect escape route from incarceration and their parents never expected a thing.

But one day one of the little fellows heard his dad say to his wife, "Honey, I think I'm going to cut down that tree beside the house because out of all these years, it has never born any fruit." He ran and told his brother about their dad's plan and together they came up with another clever plan.

They broke open their piggy banks, took the money out and hurried down to the grocery store and bought a dozen apples and a big ball of twine. They rushed home and that night they tied apples all over that tree. The next morning, they were startled when they heard their father say, "Sweetheart! It's a miracle, that tree has apples all over it!

But it's the first time I have ever seen a pear tree bear apples!"

Matthew 7:17-19 Even so every good tree bringeth forth good fruit; but a corrupt tree bringeth forth evil fruit. A good tree cannot bring forth evil fruit; neither can a corrupt tree bring forth good fruit. Every tree that bringeth not forth good fruit is hewn down, and cast into the fire.

Full Barns But Empty Soul

Can't you hear the saws buzzing? Can't you hear the hammers rapping as they drive nails into lumber? Can't you hear the hundreds of workers chatting as huge barns are being built? The rich farmer is standing there with his blueprints in his hand, monitoring the building project and ensuring that the builders are erecting the barns according to plans. Finally, the buildings are complete and rich farmer stands back with a big smile on his face admiring his beautiful work. His barns are finished and full.

Afterwards, he has a party and invites all of his friends and neighbors over to celebrate the completion of the buildings. The wine is flowing in abundance, roasted lamb with all the trimmings and steamed vegetables are served. When the party is over and the farmers' drunken neighbors are gone, the rich man puts on his silk pajamas and climbs a spiral staircase to his bedroom. He slips down between silk sheets and a soft pillow. All of a sudden, his heart begins to sputter, his breath shortens, his head spins, and he sits up in the bed. He hears a voice pounding in his head,

Luke 12:20 Thou fool, this night, thy soul is required of thee.

Give God the Glory

A little boy goes to a football game with his dad. It is the championship game for the local high school. The little boy notices that at one end of the field the football team is kneeling and praying. But, then he notices at the other end of the field the other team is also kneeling and praying as well. The little boy looked up at his dad and said, "Dad look! Both teams are praying, but I wonder how God will answer their prayer?" The father said, "What do you mean, son?" The little boy said, "Obviously they both can't win the game, who will God answer?" The father thought for a moment and said to his son, "The team that will give him the most glory."

John 5:14 And this is the confidence that we have in him, that, if we ask any thing according to his will, he heareth us:

Goals Attained Through Bended Knees

Michael Jordan is arguably the greatest basketball player who ever lived. At the height of his career he was known as "Air Jordan." He would come down the court with the basketball, begin his launch toward the goal at the foul line, and slam dunk the ball. No one in basketball history has been able to do that.

A reporter asked him about the secret of his jumping ability. The reporter asked him, "Is the secret in your shoes? Is the secret in your uniform? Do you perform some special exercise that other players don't know about to increase your leg strength?" Jordan said to the reporter, "The secret is not my shoes, nor is it my uniform, and I don't do special exercise. You see the reason I jump so high is because of what I learned back in Wilmington in high school. The lower I bend my knees, the higher I can jump towards my goal."

This is also true for a Christian. Our goals in life are within our grasp, but we must be constantly in prayer to God for help. The lower we bend our knees, the higher we can jump towards our goals.

1 John 5:14 And this is the confidence that we have in him, that, if we ask any thing according to his will, he heareth us:

Giving Myself

A young boy came to church one cold winter day to get out of the blowing snow. He had been trying to sell newspapers but not a single customer stopped because of the weather. He slipped into the back of the church, just hoping to get warm and catch up on his sleep. Though the Sunday crowd was slim, the boy really paid attention to the sermon and was greatly moved by it.

When the pastor was done, he called for the offering. The ushers went from row to row, and when the offering plate came to the boy, he stared at it for a while and then put it on the floor. He then did something very strange and very beautiful. He stood up and stepped right into the offering plate. By then, all the people had turned around and were staring at the boy. When he looked up, he had big tears running down his face as he said, "Pastor, I don't have any money because I haven't sold any newspapers today. But, if Jesus gave His life for me, then I will gladly give my life to Him." The person who has nothing to give but himself is able to give the greatest gift of all.

Mark 12:41-43 And Jesus sat over against the treasury, and beheld how the people cast money into the treasury: and many that were rich cast in much. And there came a certain poor widow, and she threw in two mites, which make a farthing. And he called unto him his disciples, and saith unto them, Verily I say unto you, That this poor widow hath cast more in, than all they which have cast into the treasury:

Giving Proves Love

There was a preacher who went to a convention in New York City. During his leisure time he went shopping for a dress for his wife. He stumbled into an expensive dress boutique, and saw a dress he thought his wife would love. He paid $500 for the dress and had it wrapped in a nice box with a card that said, "I love you so much; you mean the world to me."

When his wife opened the box and saw the dress, she looked at the card and tears rolled down her face. She took the dress, hung it up in the closet, and never wore it, but she took the card and put it on the refrigerator with a magnet. It stayed there for years. You see, God doesn't need your money, He wants you. It is not what you give in the offering, but your attitude when you give it, that's the reason why God says I love a cheerful giver! Your offering to Him always reflects your love for Him.

2 Corinthians 9:7 Every man according as he purposeth in his heart, so let him give; not grudgingly, or of necessity: for God loveth a cheerful giver.

Goats Adapt To Smell

Some college boys brought a goat into their dormitory, and the resident hall director came to visit and discovered their secret. The dorm director asked why they brought the goat into their room. "We wanted to keep him as a pet," they replied. "But what about the smell?" the manager asked. "The goat will get used to it," one boy rebutted.

Amos 4:10 I have sent among you the pestilence after the manner of Egypt: your young men have I slain with the sword, and have taken away your horses; and I have made the stink of your camps to come up unto your nostrils: yet have ye not returned unto me, saith the Lord.

God Are Good

An old retired pastor was invited to preach at a so-called elite church in his city and he gladly accepted the invitation. He stood that Sunday and in his sermon he used the phrase, "God are good." There was a young educator sitting close to the front row and supposed that the old guy simply made a mistake, but he kept saying, "God are good." The teacher was really frustrated as she thought to herself that this old man was a bad example to students in the congregation. She could hardly wait until the end of the service to reprove the old minister for his bad grammar.

After the service she walked up to the old preacher and said, "Sir in your message you repeatedly used the phrase. 'God are good' which violates subject verb agreement. The correct verb to use would be 'is' because it's used with a singular subject." The old preacher said, "Young lady, I would have used a singular verb, but God has not just blessed me singularly. He has given me plural blessings. As a matter of fact, I can't count the blessings that He has given because every time I turn around there's another blessing, God truly are good."

Nahum 1:7 The Lord is good, a stronghold in the day of trouble; and he knoweth them that trust in him.

God Has Never

God never has to apologize because he never makes a mistake.

God is never late because he is everywhere at the same time.

God doesn't think because he knows all things.

God is never caught off guard because he never sleeps.

God is never alarmed because he is all powerful.

God is never confused because he always has a plan.

God is never fearful because he is always in control.

God is never surprised because he is always ahead of the game.

2 Chronicles 16:9 For the eyes of the Lord run to and fro throughout the whole earth, to shew himself strong in the behalf of them whose heart is perfect toward him. Herein thou hast done foolishly: therefore from henceforth thou shalt have wars.

God, Give Me A Hand

An old man was riding down the road on a wagon with his son when they came to a tree that had fallen across the road. The old man said to his son, "Son, get down and move that tree out of the road." The boy tried to move the tree, but he couldn't. He went into the woods and got a huge limb and tried to use it as a lever, but he still couldn't move the tree. He struggled, pushed, pried, but to no avail.

Finally, he crawled back up into the wagon and said to his father, "I can't move the tree out of the road. I've done everything I know, but it is impossible." The old man said, "You haven't tried everything, son." The little boy said, "What did I forget?" The old man said, "You didn't ask me to give you a hand."

Matthew 7:7 Ask, and it shall be given you; seek, and ye shall find; knock, and it shall be opened unto you:

God Hears Our Voice

A young mother was traveling with her five-year- old son to visit her parents in New York. When she went through security at the airport, she looked around and discovered her son was not behind her. She panicked and went running through the airport looking for him. She ran up to a security agent and told him that her son was missing. He said he would place a call over the intercom system to see if he could find him. The young mother couldn't wait; she kept running, calling for her son. The agent followed her as she ran down the terminal. All of a sudden she said, "There he is!" The agent asked, "Where?" She said, "Over there by gate 19, crying." She ran up and hugged her son with a sigh of relief. The agent asked her, "Out of all these people talking and laughing, how could you hear him?" She said, "Sir, he's my son."

When we become a Christian, we become children of God. Just as a mother who birthed a child knows that child's voice, God knows our voice. If we cry out to Him, we will certainly get His attention.

John 10:27 My sheep hear my voice, and I know them, and they follow me:

God Is In the Audience

Soren Kierkegaard was a Danish philosopher who converted to Christianity. He said that most Christians view church like a theatrical performance. They see themselves as the audience and the people (Pastor and choir) on the stage as actors. God is off somewhere in the stellar reaches of heaven prompting the people on the stage to entertain the people in the audience. But Kierkegaard said it's actually just the opposite. The congregation is the actors. The people on the stage are the prompters, and God is the audience.

John 4:24 God is a Spirit: and they that worship him must worship him in spirit and in truth.

God Is Not Santa Clause

Jesus didn't die just so we can go to heaven; he died so that heaven will come down to us. The Lord wants to have a relationship with us. He is not just interested in religion. He shed his blood at Calvary so that we might be justified before God the Father. Don't get the idea that at your death God is going to take a sheet of paper and tally the good versus the bad. God is not Santa Clause! He died for all of your sins, past, present, and future sins.

1 Corinthians 1:9 God is faithful, by whom ye were called unto the fellowship of his Son Jesus Christ our Lord.

God Knows Your Strength

I grew up in the country and we didn't have tractors to till our soil for our crops. My dad had two mules--Carrie and Cora. Dad would hook them to a wagon filled with wood, but I noticed that he put blinders on them. Blinders were placed on the harness so they could not see anything behind. I asked one day, "Daddy why do you put blinders on the mules?" He said, "I put blinders on the mules because if they see the load that they are pulling, they won't pull it." Then he said, "If they saw the wagon, they would think that they couldn't pull it. They really don't know what they are able to pull." Isn't it good to know that God knows what we can bear even when we don't?

1 Corinthians 10:13 There hath no temptation taken you but such as is common to man: but God is faithful, who will not suffer you to be tempted above that ye are able; but will with the temptation also make a way to escape, that ye may be able to bear it.

God Owns Us

A little boy built a beautiful little boat and carried it to the edge of the river to let it sail. He carefully placed it in the water and slowly let out the string. The boat sailed away across the water. The little fellow sat in the warm sunshine, admiring the little boat that was bobbling and dancing in the water. Suddenly a strong wind blew and pushed the boat further across the river. He tried to pull it back to shore, but the string slipped out of his hand. His little boat was caught in a strong current and disappeared downstream. The boy ran along the sandy shore looking feverishly for signs of his prized possession, but the little boat was gone. For the rest of the day he searched frantically for the boat. Finally, when it was too dark to look any longer, he went home with tears in his eyes.

A few days later, on the way home from school, the boy spotted a boat just like his in a store window. He walked up closer so that he could get a better look and sure enough, it was his long lost boat. He ran into the store and said to the owner, "Mister, that's my boat in your window, I lost it in the river a few days ago, and I want it back." "I'm sorry, young fellow," said the proprietor. "Someone brought that boat in to me yesterday and I paid them good money for it. If you want it, it will cost you five dollars."

The boy ran home and broke open his piggy bank which contained exactly five dollars. He rushed back to the store and paid the man five dollars for the boat. As he walked out of the door holding the boat close to his chest, he said "Little boat I've owned you twice, the first time I owned you was when I made you with my own hands. The second time I owned you, I gave all the money I had for you." As the little boy was walking home, a group of bullies saw him alone hugging his boat. They jumped the boy, and beat him up and took his boat from him.

The boy went home and gathered up as many of his friends as he could, and they searched until they found the bad guys. They overpowered the bullies and took the boy's little boat back from them. The boy, again, hugged his boat and said, "Little boat I've owned you three times, the first time I owned you, I made you with my hands. The second time I owned you, I paid all I had to get you back, but the third time I owned you, I fought for you and recovered you from my enemy."

One day this will be the testimony of God. He has owned us thrice. The first time He owned us was when He made man with His hand. Genesis 2:7." And the Lord God formed man of the dust of the ground, and breathed into his nostrils the breath of life; and man became a living soul." The second time God owned us was when He gave all He had to redeem us John 3:16. "For God so loved the world that he gave his only begotten Son, that whosoever believeth in him should not perish, but have everlasting life." The third time He will own His church is when He will recover us from His enemy. Revelation 1:7 "Behold, he cometh with clouds; and every eye shall see him, and they also which pierced him: and all kindreds of the earth shall wail because of him." Even so. Amen.

God made us in our mother's womb and He bought us with the

death of His son Jesus and He has made it possible for us to defeat the enemy.

I Peter 1:18-21 For you know that it was not with perishable things such as silver or gold that you were redeemed from the empty way of life handed down to you from your forefathers, but with the precious blood of Christ, a lamb without blemish or defect. He was chosen before the creation of the world, but was revealed in these last times for your sake. Through him you believe in God, who raised him from the dead and glorified him, and so your faith and hope are in God." Redeemed with the precious blood of Christ! Redeemed, bought, paid the ransom, purchased with the blood of Christ, with the sacrifice of Christ on the cross! God redeems us from all our sins through Christ.

God's Hand Is Bigger Than Ours

A grandfather would often take his grandson with him to the corner store to shop with him. There was a barrel of candy right by the checkout counter. Each time the old man would get ready to check out his merchandise, the proprietor, as a gesture of appreciation, would tell the little boy to reach over into the candy barrel and grab a handful of candy. The little fellow would look up at the store owner and say, "No sir, please get the candy for me." Each time they went to the store the same thing would happen. The boy would always ask the store owner to reach in the barrel and get the candy for him.

One day the granddad asked the boy, "Why do you always refuse to reach in that barrel, but ask the store owner to get the candy for you?" The little guy said, "Poppa, that man's hand is a lot bigger than my hand, so I always get more candy when he gets it for me." God's hand is a lot bigger than ours and therefore we must trust Him to give us what we need.

Ezekiel 37:1 The hand of the Lord was upon me, and carried me out in the spirit of the Lord, and set me down in the midst of the valley which was full of bones.

The God Of Overflow

God wants to over flow our cup so the He can bless others through us! Many of us are like that rich farmer in the parable, who wanted to build larger barns. We want a bigger cup. God told Abraham in Genesis 12:1-3, "I'm going to bless you, and make you a blessing.

When I was a little boy, my Dad always drank coffee in the morning. There was something about just standing there watching my Dad eat his food. He made it look so good. When Mom poured his coffee, she filled the cup all the way to the top and some of it would spill over into the saucer. On many occasions Daddy handed the saucer to me and I sipped from the overflow. What a God we have who enjoys our fellowship!

Psalms 23:5 Thou preparest a table before me in the presence of mine enemies: thou anointest my head with oil; my cup runneth over.

God's Pencil

One of the first things I learned in school is that a pencil has two ends, a sharp point, and an eraser. One end is for writing, and the other is for erasing. When I got saved, I learned that God has a pencil, and He is looking and booking. He writes down sin with one end, but He erases by His grace with the other. The good news is that whatever sins you have committed in your past, God will erase them and make you brand new.

Ephesians 1:7 In whom we have redemption through his blood, the forgiveness of sins, according to the riches of his grace;

God's Presence

A deacon told an eight-year- old kid to go back to the study and tell the pastor that it was time to preach. The little boy went back and saw the old pastor on his knees praying. He overheard the pastor saying to God, "I've got to stand and preach this morning, please be with me." When the little boy got back to the sanctuary, the deacon asked him, "Is the pastor coming?" The boy replied, "Yes, but he is not coming alone, he's bringing the Lord with him."

Matthew 28:19-20 Go ye therefore and teach all nations, baptizing them in the name of the Father, and of the Son, and of the Holy Ghost: Teaching them to observe all things whatsoever I have commanded you. Lo, I am with you always, even unto the end of the world. Amen.

God's Protection

One day I was running in Greensboro, N.C. when I noticed that there was a house that had a sign in the yard that said, "Invisible fence." This puzzled me for a moment until I noticed a huge German shepherd in the yard. Then I realized that the owner had provided protection for pedestrians who walked past his property. I couldn't see a fence, but apparently the dog knew that he was restricted to how far he could go because of this invisible fence. You see, that dog knew his limitations, even though I couldn't see them.

God has built a hedge around us as believers and even though we can't see it, the devil can't get to us without God's permission. We have a hedge around us—a company of angels.

Job 1:10 Hast not thou made a hedge about him, and about his house, and about all that he had on every side? Thou hast blessed the work of his hands and his substance is increased in the land.

God Will Get Your Attention

The story is told about an old farmer who had a mule for sale. A perspective buyer came by one day to check out the farmer's offer. The farmer hitched the animal up to a wagon, they both sat in the seat, and the farmer handed the reins to the visitor. The man said to the mule, "Get up," but the mule just stood there. The man again said, "Get up!" The mule just looked back at them both. The man again shouted, "Get up mule!" The mule stood motionless. The farmer got down off the wagon, picked up a two by four that was lying on the ground and whacked the mule right between the eyes causing the old mule to stagger. He got back up on the wagon and said, "Now try it again." The man said, "Get up," and the mule started pulling the wagon. The prospective buyer said, "Why did you do that?" The farmer responded, "Sometimes you have to get his attention before he obeys."

God has many ways of getting our attention. Why not listen attentively to His voice before He has to whack you between your eyes with a two by four?

Jonah 1:17 Now the Lord had prepared a great fish to swallow up Jonah. And Jonah was in the belly of the fish three days and three nights.

Going Around in Circles

One of my favorite movies of all times is Groundhog Day in which Bill Murray plays a character named Phil Connors. The movie is about a man who finds himself living the same day over and over again every day. He's the only person in the world who knows this is happening, and after going through periods of dismay and bitterness, revolt and despair, suicidal self-destruction and cynical recklessness, he begins to do something that is alien to his nature. He begins to learn about himself.

Phil Connors is a weatherman who is dispensed to Punxsutawney, Pennsylvania to write a story about Groundhog Day. After doing the story he discovers that he's in a time warp. He wakes up every day at 6 o'clock, meets the same people on the street, and re-lives the same events of February 2. This movie perfectly describes the life of many of us today. It doesn't take long into a new year before many of us have already abandoned our new year's resolutions. We've made promises and decisions for change, but many of us are right back where we started. We keep going around and around in circles.

Changing is not easy. Most of us are creatures of habit, and the habits obstruct change. If you keep doing what you've been doing, you will keep getting what you've been getting. We get up at the same time every morning and eat the same breakfast. We leave home at the same time, and take the same route to work. We eat lunch at the same time and fraternize with the same people on the job under the same cantankerous supervisor. We get off work the same time, take the same route back home, eat dinner at the same time, and sit down in the same recliner. We watch the same shows over and over. We wake up at the same time in the same recliner and go to bed again at the same time. It's a vicious cycle.

Not only do our days and weeks seem to be monotonous but also our lives. Some of us are suffering from the same problems our parents and grandparents suffered with. According to Exodus 34:6, generational curses have crippled many families in our community. The same problem Granddad had, Dad is contending with. If we don't get a handle on it and stop going around in circles, our children will deal with the same thing that our parents dealt with.

Here is the good news. God has some great plans for you! You were created for a purpose. Every one of us has a special divine design. The butcher, the baker, the druggist the mechanic, the brick mason, the street sweeper, the teacher, the doctor, and the lawyer all have a divine purpose. And so do you. God does not want you living from hand to mouth, living to eat and eating to live. God wants you to make a difference. God has a Canaan for you. God has given every believer an incredible opportunity for ministry and we need to capitalize on it by breaking out of the circle.

Jeremiah 29:11 For I know the thoughts that I think toward you, saith the Lord, thoughts of peace, and not of evil, to give you an expected end.

Going to Heaven in a Lawn Chair

On July 2, 1982 Larry Walters was drinking beer in the backyard of his girlfriend's house. He fastened 42 surplus balloons to a lawn chair and launched himself from her San Pedro home. He carried various supplies with him as well as a CB radio and a BB gun to shoot balloons one at a time to descend. When he cut a rope holding him to the ground, he took off with such a jolt that another anchor rope broke under the stress and he shot upward so quickly that his eyeglasses flew to the ground.

He floated around the L.A. basin for several hours and reached altitudes of up to 16,000 feet. According to an article in the New York Times the next day, Walters was spotted by pilots from both TWA and Delta Airlines.

It was cold at 16,000 feet and he started shooting some of his balloons to descend, but dropped his BB gun, and had to wait for his rig to come down on its own. He landed in a residential neighborhood in Long Beach where got tangled in some power lines, causing a power blackout. He was asked by reporters why he did that, and his response was, "Well, you can't just sit there."

Larry tried to get to God in a lawn chair. He didn't know it but that is exactly what he was trying to do. There is a built in God-vacuum in all of us that only God can fill. It's God's breath. God breathed into Adam's nostrils the breath of life and man became a living soul. Genesis 2:7. People are trying to get to God through alcohol and drugs, materialism, addictions, sex, gambling, Internet, Facebook, Kleptomania, pyromania, food, pornography, playing video, working, and exercising. All of this is the human spirit trying to find peace for a troubled heart, but Jesus said to his disciples, "Let not your heart be troubled." The word "let" means that the ball is in our court.

John 14:6 Jesus saith unto him, I am the way, the truth, and the life: no man cometh unto the Father, but by me.

Goodness and Mercy

A crime boss had ravaged a city. He had drug dealers on every corner, gambling casinos and houses of ill-repute were sprinkled throughout the city. Prostitutes were strategically placed in locations to attract business men who came to town.

One day, a preacher came to the city and set up a tent and began preaching the Gospel. Many people were beautifully and gloriously saved. Many of the drug dealers stopped selling drugs, and the gamblers stopped rolling their dice. The prostitutes found churches in the area and became witnesses of the power of the Gospel. When the crime boss saw this, he hired a hit man to go out and kill the preacher.

One night the hit man came to the preacher's hotel room and handed him a bag filled with money. When the preacher asked what was it for the man said, "I was hired to kill you and paid this money, but every time I attempted to ambush you, there were two men following you, and I couldn't get a good shot." The preacher said, "I'm always alone and no one is with me." But the hit man said, "There are always two men with you whether you see them or not." The preacher realized what the man was saying, when he remembered:

Psalms 23:6 Goodness and mercy shall follow me all the days of my life.

Good News and Bad News

One week, the church where I was preaching assigned one of their deacons to be my driver. Each night on the way to church, we had great fellowship traveling to church for service. He was a retired truck driver and he shared a story about one of the employees where he worked who had a fearful experience.

Periodically, the trucking company gave random drug screenings to all truckers. No one would have ever suspected this particular driver to be a drug user, not even the supervisor. The boss told him that the next day they would give him a drug test. This guy went home and asked his wife to give him a specimen, and he brought it back the next day. When he was told to go get a sample, he went into the restroom, and used the one his wife gave him.

That evening, his boss called him in and said to him, "I have some good news and some bad news. The good news is you passed the pee test, the bad news is you are pregnant."

Proverbs 19:5 A false witness shall not be unpunished, and he that speaketh lies shall not escape.

Grab Him Low, and Holler for Help

In 1959 Dick Lane was called the most feared tackler in professional football. He developed a technique called the night train necktie. Back then you could hit a player in the head, which is illegal today, and clothes lining was also accepted in the game. When the Rams played the Cleveland Browns, Jim Brown had over 200 yards and no one could seem to stop him. At the end of the game they interviewed Night Train Lane, and asked him about Jim Brown's yardage that day. Night Train Lane said that the only way to tackle Jim Brown was to hit him around his feet because if you hit him up high in his face, he would run over you. The only thing you could do to stop Brown, Lane said, was to hit him around his feet, hold on, and holler for help.

This is some good advice if you want to get God's attention because if you come to him arrogantly and puffed up, you won't get a response. But what we need to do is to go down and hit him around his feet, call some prayer warriors, then holler for help.

James 4:10 Humble yourselves in the sight of the Lord, and he shall lift you up.

Grandpa's Broken Promise

A young mother invited her dad over to babysit her little daughter. The proud grandpa rushed to take the little girl out of her crib every time she cried. The mother told her father to stop taking the little girl from the crib, but the old guy couldn't resist comforting his granddaughter. Finally, the mother demanded that the old man promise that he wouldn't take the baby from her crib, to which he complied. When the baby began to cry again, she was surprised to see the old man standing in the baby's crib. She asked him what was he doing and he said, "I promised you I wouldn't take her out the crib but I didn't promise that I wouldn't get in the crib with her."

God may not take us out of the fiery furnace, but He will get in with us. God may not take us out of the lion's den, but he will get in with us. God may not take us out of trouble, but it is good to know that He will get into the trouble with us.

Matthew 28:19-20 Go ye therefore, and teach all nations, baptizing them in the name of the Father, and of the Son, and of the Holy Ghost: Teaching them to observe all things whatsoever I have commanded you: and, lo, I am with you always, even unto the end of the world. Amen.

Grasshopper and the Eagle

Your exploits in life are not dependent on how you see things nor do they depend on how others see you, but your achievements depend on how you see you. Your view of yourself is far more important than your world view. If you see yourself as a failure, you will certainly fail, if you see yourself as nobody, you will act irresponsibly and recklessly. But if you see yourself as king or queen, it will be reflected in your actions.

Ten of those twelve spies who were sent on a reconnaissance mission by Moses came back with this report, "We were in our own sight as grasshoppers in the presence of giants." (Num.13:33) We are not grasshoppers; we are eagles. All a grasshopper sees is dirt, but an eagle sees the heights of majestic splendor of God's creation.

Isaiah 40:31 But they that wait upon the Lord shall renew their strength; they shall mount up with wings as eagles; they shall run, and not be weary; and they shall walk, and not faint.

Grateful Dog

A man had a dog became ill, and he couldn't keep anything on his stomach. Soon, the dog developed the mange and was a pitiful sight to see. The man mixed a concoction, and rubbed it all over the dog's body. He also created an elixir he had learned to make from his father and put it in the dog's food. About three days later, the dog improved. He started eating and his fur returned to its original condition. The dog completely recovered from its disease.

But one day the man looked for the dog, and the dog was nowhere to be found. The dog had left home. The man couldn't believe that the dog could be so ungrateful and unfaithful after all he had done for him. A week passed: two weeks passed, but still no Rover in sight.

One day the man heard a scratch at the door. He opened the door and there was Rover, but he had seven other dogs with him. The dogs he had with him were mangy, emaciated and peeked. The man asked, "Rover after all I've done for you, why did you run away?" Rover turned to the other dogs and whimpered, as if to say, "I left so I could bring my friends who were as sick as me because I know that if you healed me, you can heal them."

Proverbs 18:24 A man that hath friends must shew himself friendly: and there is a friend that sticketh closer than a brother.

Hearing and Believing

A little girl is standing on the ledge of a burning building, and the fire is closing in behind her. A fire truck pulls up and a huge fireman rushes underneath the window and holds out his arms. He says, "Jump sweetheart, don't be afraid I'll catch you." The frightened little girl had to make a decision which illustrates faith. One part is hearing the firemen saying, "Jump!" Another part of faith is believing that the firemen is able to catch her, but the real part of faith is when she jumps off the ledge.

Real faith is seen when we not only hear the Word, but when what we hear affects our behavior.

James 2:17 Faith without works is dead.

Heaven for Willie

There was a practice in America called sharecropping. Rich people would allow poor people, mostly Black, to live on their property and in their houses in exchange for their labor on their farms. The poor people would work all year picking cotton and at the end of the year the property owner would give them a very small portion of the profits he made from the cotton.

Many of the sharecroppers would take the little money at the end of the year and go drinking and partying and spend all of it, but there was one sharecropper who would never go frolicking with his neighbors and no one knew why.

The property owner called all of them together at the end of the year and told all of them that he was selling his place and moving on. They would all have to find a new place to live. Many of them cried and wailed because they had no place to go, but they noticed that Willie was smiling. They asked him how he could be so happy when he was just told he would be put out of his house. His response was, "Remember all those years boss gave us our earnings at the end of the year? Many of you spent yours on liquor and partying, but I put mine on a house and I paid my last payment last month. So I got somewhere to go when I leave here."

2 Timothy 4:8 Henceforth there is laid up for me a crown of righteousness, which the Lord, the righteous judge, shall give me at that day: and not to me only, but unto all them also that love his appearing.

Heaven's Windows

I like windows. When I was in elementary school I always chose a seat by the window. When my family went for a ride on Sunday evening I always liked sitting by the window. I fly quite a bit and guess what? I pick the window seat. Windows have a twofold purpose. They let light in and they allow those on the inside to see outside. Did you know that heaven has windows? When we get saved we are citizens of the Kingdom. Paul says we are seated in heavenly places, but many believers can't see because there is no light coming. Many of us who are saved can't see because we don't tithe.

Malachi 3:10 I will pour you out a blessing, I will rebuke the devourer, I will protect your fruit, I will give you respect of your haters.

Heed the Warnings

There was a man who lived in South Florida in a hurricane zone. He saw a weather report that indicated a hurricane was on the way but ignored it. He saw his neighbors leaving with the valuables in the SUV's after boarding up the windows of their homes. The sheriff came out with a warning that all residents should leave, and that if he chose to stay in his home, first responders would not be dispatched to help. Again, he refused to leave his home. When the storm came it was so severe that water began to rise. He went up on top of his house and called for help. He was reminded that he had neglected three warnings, so now there was no hope.

God sends us warnings, but many of us do not heed them. The operation, the accident on the interstate, and the wrinkles on our faces, are all warnings that our time is near. Pay close attention to God's warnings while there is hope.

Isaiah 55:6 Seek ye the Lord while he may be found, call ye upon him while he is near.

He is Alive

An old farmer had one son who was serving in the military during the Vietnam War. He received word one day that his son had been killed in action. The old man plunged into deep grief and depression.

While he was mourning the loss of his only son, it was discovered that his son was still alive. A committee was dispatched to go to the old farmer's house and to tell him the good news. When they arrived at the farm the father's lip was quivering, his eyes were tear-stained, his voice was trembling but, this committee, headed by the chaplain, gave him the good news about his son!

That's what we ought to do as the Church, we should go tell a dying world that the Son is not dead. He is alive.

Matthew 28:6-7 He is not here: for he is risen, as he said. Come; see the place where the Lord lay. And go quickly, and tell his disciples that he is risen from the dead; and, behold, he goeth before you into Galilee; there shall ye see him: lo, I have told you.

He Will Help Us Across

Derick Redmond was the favorite in the 1992 Olympic Games in Barcelona, Spain. In his race, he was ahead until he pulled a hamstring in the four hundred meters semifinals. Redmond fell on the track writhing in pain when a man came out of the stands and lifted him off of the track and put his arm around him. Everyone was wondering who the man was who came to help Redmond. Some suspected it was one of his trainers or his coach, but it was later revealed that the person who came to assist Redmond was his father.

We used to sing in the old church, "Jordan River I'm bound to cross, mother will be waiting, but she can't help me to cross." But we concluded, "Jesus is waiting and he will help us across."

Joshua 3:5-7 And Joshua said unto the people, Sanctify yourselves: for tomorrow the Lord will do wonders among you. And Joshua spake unto the priests, saying, Take up the Ark of the Covenant, and pass over before the people. And they took up the Ark of the Covenant, and went before the people. And the Lord said unto Joshua, This day will I begin to magnify thee in the sight of all Israel, that they may know that, as I was with Moses, so I will be with thee.

History Lesson

He is poised at the starting line. His heart is racing with anticipation. His eyes are focused and staring in the distance down the ice course. His ears are tuned and waiting for the crack of the starting pistol to signal the start of the race. His pulse is accelerated and his breathing is intense. He hears the pop of the starter's gun, and with all his collective strength he pushes away from the starting line. His massive legs move with increased rapidity from side to side, while his body tears into the wind. His muscular arms swing from right to left, balancing his well chiseled frame as he gathers more speed while he skates in a crouched position to reduce wind resistance. Every cell, every sinew, every muscle, and every fiber of his being has been activated to perform in optimum efficiency to be the first to cross to finish line.

This is a picture of an ice racer, but it also pictures history. Some ancient sages would suggest that history is circular. They would have us believe that what goes around comes around. While that may be true, I would like to suggest also that life is not only cyclical but it is pendulous as well. Like the legs of an ice skater moves from right to left to push his body to his destiny, so does the events of history move in a pendulous fashion.

We can see this in the elections of American presidents. President Donald Trump is considered to be the 45th president, but in reality there have been only 44 presidents because Grover Cleveland was counted twice as our 22nd and 24th president because he was elected for two nonconsecutive terms. Out of the 44 presidents that we've had, 18 were Republicans and 16 were Democrats. I want to suggest that this right to left continuum has driven the American electorate since our inception. Where are we now? In 2008 it swung left, but since the rise of the Tea Party Movement, it seems to be pushing this country back towards the right. As this right-left phenomenon has driven American history, the church of Jesus Christ has remained the same. The church should espouse no political party, only the causes of Christ. We are not Republican or Democrat, right wing or Left Wing, liberal or conservative.

Hebrews 13:8 Jesus Christ the same yesterday, today and forever.

Holding Pattern

I was flying in from Denver, Colorado a few years ago into Charlotte, North Carolina. When we got to Charlotte, the captain came over the public address system and said, "We are going to have to circle the airport because there is some confusion on the ground." We circled around the airport for about 25 minutes, and everyone was concerned about the delay, but the captain came over the PA system again and said, "We have been cleared for landing. There were several planes on our runway that had to be cleared, but we will have you on the ground in just a few minutes."

We were in a holding pattern, because there were some obstructions on the ground. Somebody today is in a holding pattern because there are some obstructions on the ground. Some of us don't tithe. Some people have unforgiveness in their hearts. Some have bad attitudes toward others, and some have lying tongues they don't control. Fault finding, finger pointing, and critical spirits also will all keep us in a holding pattern and prevent us from having a safe landing at our destination.

Deuteronomy. 2:2-4 And the Lord spake unto me, saying, Ye have compassed this mountain long enough: turn you northward. And command thou the people, saying, Ye are to pass through the coast of your brethren the children of Esau, which dwell in Seir; and they shall be afraid of you: take ye good heed unto yourselves therefore:

Honest Convict

Back in the early south, there were chain gangs which consisted of men who were convicted of crimes. They would work along roads and bridges, dragging chains to keep them from escaping. Sheriffs and deputies carried shot guns and guarded them to insure public safety.

One day the governor came by to inspect work crews in a small town. He walked over to a convict and asked, "Why are you here? What was your crime?" The man said, "Sir, I just happened to be at the wrong place at the wrong time. I did nothing wrong. I was falsely accused." The governor walked over to another man who was digging a ditch, and asked the same question. His response was, "Governor, I'm an innocent man. They set me up and made me take the fall for the rest of them. I did nothing wrong."

The governor saw a third man swinging a hammer and asked, "What's your crime? Why are you here?" The man said, "Sir, I dishonored my parents and led a wicked life. I robbed people and committed crimes against the state. I was tried and justly condemned to hard labor for the evil that I have done." The governor said, "Guards come and release this man, he has no business being in the midst of such good men as these. I have a pardon waiting for him. Release him now!" All God looks for in humans is honesty, not perfection.

Romans 10:10 For with the heart man believeth unto righteousness; and with the mouth confession is made unto salvation.

Honest Joel

What would you do if you saw an envelope lying on the ground as you exited Wal-Mart containing 35 hundred crisp one hundred-dollar bills?

I was sitting at home reading when my phone rang. It was one of my members on the line. He said, "Pastor I need your help. I found a Peoples Bank Christmas envelope on the ground in front of Wal-Mart with a lot on money in it, and I don't know what to do." I asked him, "Did you go back in the store to ask if anyone reported it lost?" He said, "No because I was so afraid." The caller is a very bashful 76-year- old widower who lives by himself and a faithful member of our church. I told him, "Give me a few minutes, and I'll call you back." I needed to do a little investigation.

I called the Peoples Bank and introduced myself as pastor and gave her the details of my conversation. She said there was no way to find out who the money belonged to unless she knew the exact amount. I called Joel back and told him to count the money. He was so nervous that up this point he had not even counted it. He told me that it was new money, "sticking together" and that it would take him a while to count it. So, I asked him to count the money and call me back.

A few minutes later he called and gave me the amount, $3500.00. I called the bank representative and gave her the amount. There are several Peoples Bank locations in my city, but when I told her $3500.00, she immediately identified the location where the money was dispensed. She said the bank would contact the lady and get back with me.

I called the church member, told him the good news, and asked him if he wanted me to take him down to the bank. He said, "Pastor just come by and get the money and take for me." I told him I wanted him to go with me so that you could meet the woman who lost the money."

When we arrived at the bank, a lady behind the bank counter walked from behind the counter and greeted us. She pointed to an older white lady whose eyes were red with tears sitting in the lobby. Then she said, "This is the lady who lost the money." The woman literally ran towards us, not even looking at the envelope that he was extending towards her. She hugged him like he was her own brother. With tears streaming down her blushed face and with a cracking voice, she kept saying, "Thank you!" The member was embarrassed, so he pointed towards me and said to the grateful woman, "This is my pastor." She turned from him and started hugging me. Everyone in the bank had tuned in to our conversation. The woman told us that her crippled sister was in the car and she wanted us to meet her.

When we walked outside, her sister had found the strength to get out of the van. She began hugging us as her face filled with tears. Bank customers were arriving probably wondering, why there were two white women crying and hugging two big black guys? We wished them a Merry Christmas, got in my car, and headed back towards his house.

As we left the bank, I noticed that those two ladies were not the only ones crying. There was a tear rolling down his face as he looked over at me and said, "I couldn't have slept a wink knowing that I had someone else's money in my house." I thought to myself, this is truly a man of God, one who takes his confession of faith seriously. I wish there were more people like him in the world.

1 Thessalonians 4:12 That ye may walk honestly toward them that are without, and that ye may have lack of nothing.

I Came to See Jesus

In 2008, candidate Barack Obama was running for president and his pastor was Jeremiah Wright. Wright had said some awful things about America and the media had a frenzy over it. Fox News showed up at Jeremiah Wright's church one morning to interview some of the members of his church.

Many worshippers were walking in the back door of the church to avoid speaking to the media. But there was one old mother who walked directly up to the camera. A reporter extended his microphone towards her and said, "Why do you come to this church? Do you know that this man has maligned this country? Haven't you heard the things Mr. Wright has said about America? How could you worship in such a place with this man as acting pastor?" That old woman looked directly into the camera and said, "I did not come here to see Jeremiah Wright. I came to see Jesus."

This should be the attitude of every church goer. Never go to church to see the pastor. Go to church to see Jesus.

John 12:21 The same came therefore to Philip, which was of Bethsaida of Galilee, and desired him, saying, Sir, we would see Jesus.

I Forgive You

He walked into Mother Emanuel AME Church and sat through Bible study with nine members who showed up that night. At the end of the service he pulled out a handgun and killed all nine people who were in attendance, including the pastor Clementa Pinckney. At the hearing, Nadine Collier, the daughter of 70-year-old Ethel Lance who was killed in the shooting said, "I forgive you," her voice breaking with emotion. "You took something very precious from me. I will never talk to her again. I will never, ever hold her again. But I forgive you. And have mercy on your soul." If she could forgive Roof, why can't you forgive the person who cut you off in traffic?

Ephesians 4:32 And be ye kind one to another, tenderhearted, forgiving one another, even as God for Christ's sake hath forgiven you.

If You Only Knew Where I've Been

A man from Alaska boarded a plane with a fur coat, a wool sweater, and leather boots because it was 30 degrees. He flew to Miami, Florida for a business meeting, but when he got off the plane, people stared and giggled because of how he was dressed. He overheard someone say, "Look at him. It's 100 degrees, and this idiot is dressed like it's winter. One guy walked up to him and said, "Hey, fellow, you must be burning up in all those clothes. Do you know that it is a hundred degrees here?" The traveler smiled and answered, "Sir, I know where I am, but you don't know where I've been. If you knew where I came from, you would understand why I'm dressed this way. I hear people making fun of me and telling jokes, but it's because they don't know from where I came." You can tell where people came from by their praise and their worship.

Acts 3:7-9 And he took him by the right hand and lifted him up: and immediately his feet and ankle bones received strength. And he leaping up stood, and walked, and entered with them into the temple, walking, and leaping, and praising God.

I Have a Song

When peace like a river attendeth my way,
When sorrows like sea billows roll,
Whatever my lot, Thou hast taught me to say,
It is well; it is well with my soul.
It is well with my soul,
It is well; it is well with my soul. Horatio G. Spafford (1828-1888)

This is just one of many hymns in our hymnbook that was written on the backdrop of pain and sorrow. If I attempted to enumerate all of the hymn writers who penned hymns while dealing with sorrow, it would be too large of a discourse for any sermon. As a matter of fact, if you would examine the Book of Psalms, the Old Testament hymnbook, you will discover that many of those hymns were written while its authors were struggling with deep, dark, spiritual and physical agony. What gave them the unusual ability to sing in the midst of sorrow? It was their faith in God. Someone has said, "A bird sitting on a tree is never afraid of the branch breaking because her trust is not on the branch but on its own wings. Maya Angelou once wrote, "A bird doesn't sing because it has an answer, it sings because it has a song."

Ephesians 5:19 Speaking to yourselves in psalms and hymns and spiritual songs, singing and making melody in your heart to the Lord;

I've Got Sunshine

The late Dr. Sandy Ray tells a story about his first year in Morehouse College in Atlanta, Georgia. He said at the end of the semester he had no money to pay tuition, no money to buy books, he didn't even have lunch money. He did not know how he would pay the first semester, and he could not see any means to take care of the second semester.

One day it was gloomy physically, mentally and spiritually. The sun was not shining, and there was a fog on campus. Dr. Ray recounts that while he was feeling down he overheard a voice on the outside of his door, and he decided to investigate. He walked outside and saw a homeless man ransacking a trash bin, but while he was rambling through the garbage he was singing a song. He was singing "I've got sunshine on a cloudy day, when it's cold outside it's like the month of May. I guess you've said it, what can make me feel this way, my girl, talking about my girl." Dr. Ray said to himself, "If a guy who doesn't even have food on his table, a decent change in clothes or a place to sleep can sing in his condition, what about me?" He started singing, "Why do I feel discouraged, and why do the shadows come, why does my heart feel lonely and long for heaven as home. When Jesus is my portion and a constant friend is he, his eye is on the sparrow and know he's watching me."

Colossians 3:16 Let the word of Christ dwell in you richly in all wisdom; teaching and admonishing one another in psalms and hymns and spiritual songs, singing with grace in your hearts to the Lord.

I'll Alter Him

During the rehearsal for her wedding a nervous bride was having a difficult time remembering all the details. Her kind pastor took her aside at the end of the night and said, "When you enter the church tomorrow, you will be walking down the same aisle you've walked down many times before. Concentrate on the aisle. And when you get halfway down the aisle, concentrate on the altar. And, when you reach the end of the aisle, your groom will be waiting for you. Concentrate on him. Focus on the aisle, then look at the altar, and finally, lock eyes with your man. That's all you have to do."

That seemed to help a lot, and on the day of the wedding, the beautiful, but nervous bride walked flawlessly down the aisle. But people were a bit taken aback as they heard her repeating these words during the processional, "Aisle, alter, him. Aisle, alter, him. (I'll alter him)." An old lady sitting in the corner of the chapel blurted out, "No you won't. If his Mama couldn't change him, you sure can't."

2 Corinthians 6:13-15 Now for a recompense in the same, (I speak as unto my children,) be ye also enlarged. Be ye not unequally yoked together with unbelievers: for what fellowship hath righteousness with unrighteousness? And what communion hath light with darkness? And what concord hath Christ with Belial? Or what part hath he that believeth with an infidel?

I'm Packing Heat

I was criticized for hosting concealed weapons permit classes a couple of years ago. As a matter of fact, we lost some members because of it. Why should Christians own guns, was their argument. But the Bible gives a man the responsibility to not only provide for his family but to protect them as well. So, if a man owns a gun to protect his family, he needs to be correctly trained to do so. I was glad I had that training because one day I was at my Mom's house in a huge field with my weapon on my side. Suddenly a pack of growling dogs came rushing towards me, and I quickly pulled my pistol and fired several rounds into the ground close to them. They scattered back into the woods. If I hadn't been carrying my heat, there's no telling what those dogs would have done to me.

Well, God has given the church some heat. He's called the Holy Ghost, and when the devil attacks, he has to respect our heat. Tell someone close to you, "I'm packing heat!"

Acts 1:8 But ye shall receive power, after that the Holy Ghost is come upon you: and ye shall be witnesses unto me both in Jerusalem, and in all Judaea, and in Samaria, and unto the uttermost part of the earth.

I'm Still Here

One of my favorite scenes in the movie "The Color Purple" is when Celie is about to leave Mister who had consistently abused her for years. He had humiliated her and used her as a mere servant and called her all sorts of names, but she was leaving him for the last time. She walked off the porch to get into the awaiting automobile and Mister chased after her with his hand elevated as if he was going to slap her. Celie stuck out two fingers and said, "Whatever you have done to me is already done to you." She then climbed into the car and as the car was driving off, she looked back at him and said, "I'm poor, black, I may even be ugly, but Dear God, I'm here! I'm here!" We can say the same thing to our haters and even the devil. All you tried to do to us will ultimately happen to you. And we may not have had everything we wanted, but we are still here.

Mark 4:37-41 And there arose a great storm of wind, and the waves beat into the ship, so that it was now full. And he was in the hinder part of the ship, asleep on a pillow and they awake him, and say unto him, Master, carest thou not that we perish? And he arose, and rebuked the wind, and said unto the sea, Peace, be still. And the wind ceased, and there was a great calm. And he said unto them, why are ye so fearful? How is it that ye have no faith? And they feared exceedingly, and said one to another, what manner of man is this, that even the wind and the sea obey him?

Introductions are Always Needed

Sometimes when I'm doing revivals or getting ready to preach in another pulpit, the person who is introducing me will say, "He needs no introduction." I know that they are trying to be kind and flattering, but I always think to myself, everyone needs an introduction. For years Ed McMahon would say, "Here's Johnny!" The announcer on The Price is Right, says, "Come on down!" When fighters are getting ready for their big fight, the Johnny Buffer says, "Let's get ready to rumble! In this corner..." As famous as the President of the United States is, he always receives an introduction. "Ladies and gentlemen, the President of the United States." John's introduction of Jesus was, "Repent for the Kingdom of heaven is at hand."

Matthew 17:12-13 But I say unto you, That Elias is come already, and they knew him not, but have done unto him whatsoever they listed. Likewise shall also the Son of man suffer of them. Then the disciples understood that he spake unto them of John the Baptist.

It Has To Cost You Something

I begged for a bike when I was a kid, but my dad never bought it for me. Instead he allowed me to pick peaches, mow lawns and cut wood to earn $7.50 to buy my first bike. I wanted a car when I was 16, but my dad never bought it for me. Instead he sent me to work at a filling station changing tires for a whole year to earn $400 to buy my 56 Chevy. I thought my dad was the meanest guy in the world when I was growing up, but now I understand what he was doing. Anything that doesn't cost us, we don't value. It has to cost you something for you to really appreciate it.

A little boy brought a beautiful bouquet of flowers one day to his mother, but the bouquet had been picked from the flower bed of a lady who lived along the route on his way home from school. His mother did not accept the flowers. She sent the little boy back to the lady's house and made him give it back to her with an apology.

The lady was very gracious and kind about it, and tried to say it was okay, but the little boy's mother would not allow it. The mother told her son that he had a personal responsibility to give what was his, not what was someone else's.

2 Samuel 24:24 And the king said unto Araunah, Nay; but I will surely buy it of thee at a price: neither will I offer burnt offerings unto the Lord my God of that which doth cost me nothing.

It's Coming To Pass

A small country church met one evening and had what they called a scripture shower. Everyone stood and recited a verse and gave the chapter and verse of the scripture they presented. One by one they stood and verbalized the memory verses, but there was one old lady who stood in the meeting and said, "Pastor, I have a favorite verse, but I don't know where it is." The pastor said, "How is it that you have a favorite verse, but you don't know where it's found in the Bible?" The only lady said, "Well pastor, it is found in a lot of places in the Bible because my favorite verse is, "It came to pass."

That nice car is coming to pass

That beautiful skin is coming to pass

That beautiful figure is coming to pass

That huge bank account is coming to pass

That palatial home is coming to pass

That beautiful family is coming to pass

Your health and strength is coming to pass

That sharp mind is coming to pass

Heaven and Earth shall pass away but my Word shall stand forever.

Matthew 6:18-20 That thou appear not unto men to fast, but unto thy Father which is in secret: and thy Father, which seeth in secret, shall reward thee openly. Lay not up for yourselves treasures upon earth, where moth and rust doth corrupt, and where thieves break through and steal: But lay up for yourselves treasures in heaven, where neither moth nor rust doth corrupt, and where thieves do not break through nor steal:

It's Too Soon to Quit

Comedian Victor Borge tells the story of his uncle and his creative pursuits to invent a soft drink. His uncle, according to Borge, sold all he had and invested in this pursuit. His efforts failed. He then auctioned off his house and for a second time, he failed. Then he borrowed from his relatives, and for a third time he failed. He sought out friends and investors and failed. He tried six times and failed to invent a soft drink. He gave up, Victor says, and died penniless. After his uncle's death, another man came along and took his formula, made one effort and invented 7Up. Victor Borge said, "You know how close my uncle came to success? He was six up."

Well, some of us are six up and about to quit. It's too soon to quit. Many of us have been praying for a family member to get saved, and it seems like the more you pray the worse they get. Consequently, you're ready to quit. Don't. It's too soon to quit. Some of us have been praying for healing of our bodies, but the more you pray the more medicine the doctor prescribed. Still, it's too soon to quit. Others of us have been praying for a home for your family, but it doesn't seem like it's anywhere in sight. You are ready to quit, but it is too soon to quit. Some may be struggling in school. You've tried for years to get that degree, but those tests keep getting worse and worse and you want to quit. It's too soon to quit. There may be somebody who is ready to give up your assignment in ministry. Maybe you are usher, or a trustee, a deacon, or an ambassador or you could be a preacher who is frustrated, despondent, and dissatisfied with the work, and you want to quit.

It is too soon to quit. Maybe you have a child that you have brought up in the fear and admonition of the Lord. You invested time and money and your life's blood into this individual, but he still in and out of jail and you want to quit. It's too soon to quit. It could be that your marriage is on the rocks, and you had a place where you say I just can't take it anymore. It is too soon to quit. You never lose until you quit.

Galatians 6:9 And let us not be weary in well doing: for in due season we shall reap, if we faint not.

It's What's Inside That Counts

Susan Boyle stepped up on the stage at the American Idol Show, and they laughed at her because she didn't look like an idol. She didn't have the glitz and splendor of an idol. Her dress was old and worn. Her hair seemed old fashioned, and people actually began to boo her before she opened her mouth because of her appearance. Simon sneered and with his usual arrogant, insensitive, and pretentious nature, he practically insulted Miss Boyle. When she began to sing, jaws dropped, eyes opened wide and people sat up and gave attention to a beautiful voice.

We often judge people by outward appearance, but it's what on the inside that counts.

1 Samuel 16:7 But the Lord said unto Samuel, Look not on his countenance, or on the height of his stature; because I have refused him: for the Lord seeth not as man seeth; for man looketh on the outward appearance, but the Lord looketh on the heart.

I've Got A Secret

In the movie "Coming to America," Eddie Murphy plays the part of a wealthy prince (Akeem) who comes to America to find a bride. He comes with his trusted friend Semmi who aids him in keeping his identity a secret because he is afraid people will treat him differently if they know he is African royalty. He is a prince, but he doesn't want anyone to know it. What a tragedy to be royalty and want to keep it a secret. As believers, we need to understand that we are of royal decent, but Satan wants to keep it a secret.

Romans 1:16 For I am not ashamed of the gospel of Christ: for it is the power of God unto salvation to everyone that believeth; to the Jew first, and also to the Greek.

Jesus Loves Me This I Know

A senior pastor was retiring after 50 years of loyal service to his church and community. He had served faithfully in ministry, not only at his church, but also his community. He came to the area as a young man and worked his way through college and seminary. He had held the position of moderator of the local association and president of the state convention. He was well respected, both among his peers, and his people. When it was time for retirement, the church decided to give him a retirement celebration. All the dignitaries of the city were present at this grand affair, including state officials.

At the conclusion of the ceremony, the Master of Ceremony asked the old pastor to come and give some remarks. He then said, "Pastor, will you tell us younger ministers what was the comforting and consoling lesson that you learned during your long tenure as a servant of the community and church?" The old guy walked up to the mic and said these words, " Jesus loves me this I know. For the Bible tells me so. Little ones to him belong. They are weak, but he is strong. Yes, Jesus loves me. Yes, Jesus loves me, Yes, Jesus loves me, for the Bible tells me so. With that, the old guy went back to his seat.

John 15:13 Greater love hath no man than this that a man lay down his life for his friends.

Job

Job was filthy rich. Warren Buffet, Mark Zuckerberg, and Bill Gates pale in comparison to Job. The Book of Job opens by giving Job's financial portfolio, and it is an impressive one. He owned 7000 sheep, 3000 camels, 500 oxen. If a man owned one ox in Job's day he was considered to be rich. Job had 1000 oxen because the text says he had 500 yokes of oxen. He had a beautiful family of 10 children, seven sons and three daughters. His wife took milk baths whenever she wanted to. They had servants who catered to their every whim and a community of admiring friends and neighbors. Job had everything a man could possibly want that would make him happy and comfortable.

But one day something happened that Job was not aware of. There was a meeting between Satan and God and the Lord gave the devil permission to afflict Job. Job had no idea what was going on. We have the Book of Job, but Job did not. Job went to bed one night a millionaire and woke up a pauper. He went to sleep on top of the world and woke up with the world on top of him. One bad thing happened after another. As fast as one messenger came, another came with news of destruction. Sometimes life can blind side you and catch you off guard.

If you are doing well today, enjoy it because we all are just one text from trouble. We are only one phone call from calamity and one doctor's visit from devastation. You may have the world in a jug and the stopper in your hand today, but tomorrow you may be in the jug. Sometimes trouble will come as a result of our own wrong doing, but often God tests His children by allowing trouble to come in their lives. Stand firm, it's only a test.

Job 42:5 I have heard of thee by the hearing of the ear: but now mine eye seeth thee.

Joshua Made the Moonshine

A Sunday school teacher was teaching from the Book of Joshua. The passage she was explaining was the section where Joshua prayed for enough time to defeat his enemy and God made the sun stand still. She said to the class, "Joshua was in a valley and made the sun still." A little boy blurted out, "That's nothing, my uncle Joshua is in prison because he made the moonshine."

Joshua 10:13 And the sun stood still, and the moon stayed, until the people had avenged themselves upon their enemies. Is not this written in the book of Jasher? So the sun stood still in the midst of heaven, and hasted not to go down about a whole day.

Keeping Them Straight

A preacher quit the ministry after twenty years and became a funeral director. When asked why he changed, he said: "I spent four years trying to straighten out Bob, and Bob is still an alcoholic. Then I spent ten months trying to straighten out Judy's marriage and she filed for divorce anyway. Then I spent two years trying to straighten out Jim's drug problem and he's still an addict. Now at the funeral home when I straighten them out, they stay straight!"

Ecclesiastes 9:5 For the living know that they shall die: but the dead know not anything, neither have they any more a reward; for the memory of them is forgotten.

Keep it Real

A young woman claims that she accidentally sent a nude picture to her father, prompting him to become enraged, come to her apartment, and bang on her door as he shouted obscenities at her. She says that she was attempting to send the pictures to someone named Dequan and accidentally sent it to her dad instead. Now, she is looking for a reality TV show deal which may be the reason for these claims in the first place.

Some analysts believe that she made her story up to cash in on the reality TV phenomenon. Reality TV has exploded to the top ratings in the past few years. You can find reality shows ranging from law-enforcement, lifestyle change, fantasies fulfilled, docu-soaps starring celebrities, hidden video cameras, game shows, playoffs, talent searches, and even ice truckers.

The reason for the rise in popularity is because our culture is set on "Keeping it real." When I was a boy, TV consisted of mainly cowboy shows, "Laramie," "Gunsmoke," and "The Virginian," with a few sit coms, and cop shows sprinkled here and there. In today's climate of thrill seeking realists, that kind of programming would not suit their amusement palate. When they say, "Keep it real," I think it is an expression of a desire for truth. People today want truth.

Our culture is tired of being jerked around by the imagination of others. They are sick of being fed pseudo stories contrived in a vacuum of an altered mind fixated on personal aggrandizement. People are saying give me truth. The greatest truth ever heard is actually in the Scripture.

John 3:16 For God so loved the world, that he gave his only begotten Son, that whosoever believeth on him should not perish, but have everlasting life.

King in My Corner

We went to eat at Cracker Barrel one day, and when I came out of the restaurant, two of my granddaughters were playing checkers on the front porch. Both Elissa and Elizabeth were sitting, staring at the checkerboard. Elissa appeared to be in deep thought because it was her next move.

I looked down at the checkerboard, and I noticed that she had a king in the corner. She seemed to be puzzled about what move to take, and I said to her, "Sweetheart, you got a king in your corner." She started smiling because she knew she would win the game since she had a king in her corner. We can be happy, too, because we got "The

King" in our corner.

Revelation 1:5 And from Jesus Christ, who is the faithful witness, and the first begotten of the dead, and the prince of the kings of the earth. Unto him that loved us, and washed us from our sins in his own blood.

Know Your Purpose

A pastor was teaching his Vacation Bible School kids, and he asked them a series of questions. He asked them the purpose of a cow. They said to give milk. He asked them the bird's purpose. They said to fly in the sky. He asked them the purpose of a fish. They said "to swim in the water." Then he asked them their purpose, and one of the little boys said, "to play." It's too bad that many people never grow out of that same mentality.

Romans 8:29 For whom he did foreknow, he also did predestinate to be conformed to the image of his Son, that he might be the firstborn among many brethren.

Lackadaisical Commitment

A young man was writing his fiancée a love letter. In the letter he was declaring his undying love and unwavering commitment to her. He said in the letter, "I will climb the highest mountain. I will walk through the lowest valley. I will endure the parching hot sun of the desert, just to look on your beautiful face. I will fight off the wildest animals of the jungle, and rebuke sickness and disease from my body. I will give my life savings, just to hear you're lovely voice, because I'm yours forever." But, at the end of the letter he wrote this, P.S. I will see you Sunday evening if it's not raining.

2 Timothy 4:10 For Demas hath forsaken me, having loved this present world, and is departed unto Thessalonica; Crescens to Galatia, Titus unto Dalmatia.

Last Seen Reaching for the Top

In 1953, Sir Edmund Hillary of Great Britain was the first man to climb Mount Everest. He had faced death, danger, discouragement, and disappointment, but finally he was approaching the crest of the highest mountain in the world. The news media from all over the world was there to record Hillary as he hoisted the British flag on top of Mount Everest. But prior to his arrival to the summit of the mountain he encountered a dense fog. The cameras lost sight of Hillary as he was going through the fog and one news report out of Great Britain ran this headline, "He Was Last Seen Reaching for the Top." Faith causes us to reach for the top. Reach for holiness, happiness, wholesomeness, success, prosperity, integrity, perfection, maturity, joy, peace, love, and gentleness. If you would choose an epitaph for your life at you homegoing, shouldn't it be "He/she was last seen reaching for the top?"

Philippians 3:14 I press toward the mark for the prize of the high calling of God in Christ Jesus.

Learning Through Experience, Example, and Exposure

A little boy came home from his first day at school. His mother asked him, "Well, what did you learn today?" He said, "Not enough. They want me to come back tomorrow." Don't you wish that we could learn all we need to know about the world in one day in school? We all have to continue to go back and learn.

The truth is, even once we get out of school we should still be engaged in the learning process. A college education never hurt anyone who was willing to learn after they got it. If we stop learning, reading, and dreaming, we will dry up and die, so to speak. This is especially true when it comes to learning about God and His Word. Life is a learning process and when we stop attempting to learn, we cease to be. How do we know something? We must learn it. How do we learn something? We learn and know through experience and exposure.

When I was nine years old, my grandfather would take me to church every Sunday. I remember one day I went over to drive him to church He let me drive because that was his way of getting me interested in church. I didn't have a necktie on and he told me to watch him. He stood in front of me and I watched him tie a single Winsor knot in his tie. Then he placed a tie around my neck and said, "Now you do what I just did." He watched as I tied my first tie and I have been tying knots ever since. I can tie a tie because I have experience tying ties. I had an example; I was exposed to tying a tie; therefore, I can tie a neck tie.

Proverbs 22:6 Train up a child in the way he should go: and when he is old, he will not depart from it.

Let Go and Trust God

A man was traveling around a mountain side on the wagon when his wagon overturned. The man was thrown over a cliff but he managed to grab hold to a bush that was protruding out of the side of the mountain. He was holding onto that bush for dear life crying at the top of his lungs asking whether anyone else was up there. His hands were almost raw; his arms were numb, and his pulse was racing. He kept crying, "Help, is there anyone out there!" Finally, he heard a voice saying, "Yes, I'm here. I will help you, but you have to trust me. The man said, "What should I do?" The voice said, "Let go of the bush." The man cried, "Is there anyone else up there?" Finally, he let go of the bush only to discover that there was a ledge right under his feet.

Psalms 37:5 Commit thy way unto the Lord; trust also in him; and he shall bring it to pass.

Letter To Jesus

There was an eight-year-old girl named Bernice who lived with her widowed grandmother in a shotgun house in a small town. One cold winter, the grandmother ran out of money, and they had no groceries in the house. The lights were also turned off, and there was no heat to warm them. The little girl remembered what she was taught in Sunday school, so she sat down and wrote a letter to Jesus. "Dear Jesus, I learned in church that you would prepare a table for your children. Well, Jesus my grandmother and I are hungry. We have no lights and no heat so we are in the dark and we are cold. Please stop by and help us." Signed Bernice. She addressed it to heaven and took the letter to the mailbox.

When the postman saw the letter, he took it to his supervisor. His boss decided to open the letter thinking it was a joke. When he finished reading the letter, tears rolled down his face. He showed the letter to others at the post office, and they all decided to take up an offering. When the money was collected, the supervisor went down to the power company, and paid their light bill for Bernice's grandmother. He stopped by the grocery store and bought food and took it to the little girl's house.

When little Bernice arrived home from school, she smelled food cooking in the kitchen, and when she walked into the house, she saw that the lights were on. The postman arrived the next day and saw another letter addressed to heaven from little Bernice. " Lord, I just want to say thank you for the food on our table, the heat and lights in our house. You truly prepared a table for your children."

Genesis 22:14 And Abraham called the name of that place Jehovah Jireh: as it is said to this day, In the mount of the Lord it shall be seen.

Life on the Potter's Wheel

The potter has to rip the clay out of the ground. Then he takes it back to his potter's shack and separates the pliable clay from the non-pliable clay. He puts it on a wheel and spins it and shapes it into a vessel that he wants. Then he puts it into the oven and bakes it. If clay could talk it would tell us that this process is uncomfortable, but it is necessary to become a beautiful vessel. God often puts us through some uncomfortable situations and circumstances, but when He is through, we shall be a beautiful vessel for the Master's work.

Jeremiah 18:1-3 The word which came to Jeremiah from the Lord, saying, Arise, and go down to the potter's house, and there I will cause thee to hear my words. Then I went down to the potter's house, and, behold, he wrought a work on the wheels.

Light of the World

I want to high jack your imagination for a few moments and invite you to step into a time machine. Let's go back in time, past the hot winds of the sixties. We are going back, further than the Industrial Revolution, back beyond the Protestant Reformation. Let's go back past the Crusades of Spain and England. Let's move past the birth of Jesus at Bethlehem. We are moving further back past the birth of Moses, past the pyramids of Ramses the Second pharaoh of Egypt. Let's go all the way back to the beginning of time, the first day, the first hour, the first minute, the first second. What do you see? Nothing. It's dark, pitch black, so dark you can feel it on your face. It's darker than a thousand midnights. What do you hear? You hear the splashing of water, because the Earth is covered with water, and without form and empty. Suddenly you hear a voice, which says "Let there be light!" And in an instant light tears into the darkness, ripping it apart, at the speed of 186,280 miles per second. Now the watery abyss can be seen clearly because of the light. And then God says, "That's good." And He called the light day and darkness night.

112

Now let's fast forward back to an event in the ministry of Christ where the Pharisees had brought a women who was taken in adultery. Jesus had astutely adjudicated the case by saying to them in John 8:7, "He that is without sin among you, let him first cast a stone at her." Being condemned in their own hearts, they walked away one by one, from the oldest to the youngest. Then Jesus pivoted to the woman and said, "Woman, where are those thine accusers? Hath no man condemned thee?" She said, "No man, Lord." And Jesus said unto her, "Neither do I condemn thee. Go, and sin no more. Then spake Jesus again unto them, saying, "I am the light of the world. He that followeth me shall not walk in darkness, but shall have the light of life." Just as he spoke in creation and illuminated the dark Earth, he speaks today to illuminate the dark minds and spirits of men and women.

Life can be broken down into what are called trophic levels. You might think of this as the circle of life. In the first trophic level plants absorb energy from the sun and create nutrients. In the second level an animal, like a squirrel, eats that plant and gets the nutrients. In the third trophic level an animal eats the animal that ate the plant and in turn gets the nutrients. Here you have a wolf. Finally in the fourth tropic level you have an animal that eats the animal that ate the animal that ate the plant. A lion would fall into this grouping. All trophic levels of life depend on the energy that comes from the plant that was created by light. Without the plant's production of nutrients the whole ecosystem would fail. So without light, the plant would not produce nutrients, no nutrients in plants, no squirrel, no squirrel, no wolf, no wolf no lion. Light is necessary for life. Jesus is truly the Light of the World.

John 8:12 Then spake Jesus again unto them, saying, I am the light of the world: he that followeth me shall not walk in darkness, but shall have the light of life.

Long-winded Preaching

A little girl is sitting beside her mother on Sunday morning when the preacher pulls out a watch and lays it on the lectern. The little girl says to her mother, "Mom what does that mean?" The mother said to the little girl, "Sweetie that means nothing except that he will be up there all day."

A little boy is sitting beside his dad one Sunday morning, and the preacher is going on and on with his sermon. The little boy says, "Dad if we just give him the money now, will he let us go?"

A preacher is standing in the pulpit on Sunday morning, and he is going on and on with his message. He says to the congregation, "I'm closing now," but he continues preaching another 15 minutes. After about another 30 minutes, the preacher says to the congregation, "Is there a clock in this church so that I can gauge the length of my sermon?" An old mother in the amen corner says, "No there is no clock in the sanctuary, but there is a calendar on the wall."

Acts 20:9 And there sat in a window a certain young man named Eutychus, being fallen into a deep sleep: and as Paul was long preaching, he sunk down with sleep, and fell down from the third loft, and was taken up dead.

Loose Connection

When I was in high school, I had a 56 Chevrolet. It was green and yellow with keystone mag wheels with white lettered tires. It had a three on the floor and dual exhaust with Thrush mufflers to let everyone know I was coming. It also had a Pioneer 8 tract tape player, Hurst shifter, 265 engine and two-barrel carburetor. I'm trying to tell you, it was bad.

One day after school it wouldn't start, needless to say I was totally embarrassed. I couldn't figure out what was wrong with it. The other kids began to laugh when several of my friends had to push me off. I can still remember the faces of those kids making fun of me because my whip was broken.

When I got home, I told my dad what happened and he opened the hood and cleaned off the battery cables. He told me to get inside and turn the switch. To my amazement, my car started. Dad said, "Your car wouldn't start because you had a loose connection; therefore, you had no power."

Many Christians today have a loose connection, so there is no power. Why don't you determine today that you are going to get connected so you can have power to live life to the fullest?

Revelation 3:16 So then because thou art lukewarm, and neither cold nor hot, I will spew thee out of my mouth.

Lord, I Thank You

A national convention was held in a certain city and pastors from all over the country were invited to come and pray. One by one the pastors paraded across the stage to give their prayer. Many preachers prayed long eloquent prayers using words that most people in the audience didn't know. Suddenly, an old 90 year old preacher slowly came up to the roster with his walking cane. Many in the congregation were concerned about him even getting to the lectern.

The old man said, "Bow your heads with me please," Then he said, "Lord, thank you, thank you, thank you, thank you." The people in the audience began to raise their heads and wonder if perhaps the old guy was suffering from dementia. Even the president of the convention lifted his head and beckoned to one of his assistants to go and retrieve the old guy because everyone thought he was making a fool out of himself.

The president of the convention walked over to the senior minister and said, "Reverend, are you okay? All you're saying is thank you." The old preacher responded, "Every time I think of a blessing God had given me, it's worthy of a "thank you." God helped me raise my family on a janitor's salary. That's worth a "thank you." None of my children went to jail. That's worth a "thank you." He kept me in my right mind when my wife died. That surely is worth a "thank you." I thought about so many things that God has done and all I can do is to tell Him "thank you." Soon everyone in the congregation was saying, "Lord, thank you."

Colossians 2:7 Rooted and built up in him, and stablished in the faith, as ye have been taught, abounding therein with thanksgiving.

Lord You Are Welcome

The jury is in. Every Christian ought to be a thankful person, no if ands or buts. The words, 'Thank you Lord should fall liberally from our lips, as pollen from stems of shaken lilies. The Bible is crystal clear on this issue. We should give thanks to God at all times for all things. A healthy Christian is a thankful Christian.

I have a friend who often says, 'Thank you Lord' a hundred times. Our conversation is punctuated with carefully interjected, "Thank you, Lord!" Did you know that we should also say, "Lord, you're welcome." Two phrases should dominate our vocabulary--Thank you, Lord and Lord, you're welcome. Do you know why we have so much trouble in our home? It's because the Lord is not welcome. Do you know why there is so much trouble in our schools? It's because the Lord is not welcome. Do you know why the church is so cold you can ice skate down the aisles? It's because the Lord is not welcome.

Luke 8:40 And it came to pass, that, when Jesus was returned, the people gladly received him: for they were all waiting for him.

Love in Concrete

For 50 years a pastor preached on a theme of Christian love. Every sermon from his pulpit on Sunday morning somehow centered on the theme of Christian love. His favorite scripture was John 3:16, "For God so loved the world that he gave his only begotten son that whosoever believeth in him shall not perish but have everlasting life." It didn't matter if it was Thanksgiving, Christmas, or Easter. He somehow weaved his sermon around the theme of Christian love.

The years passed and the old preacher decided that he would retire from pastoring. The first project he undertook after retiring was excavating his driveway. After building the form for the concrete he called in the concrete trucks to come to his house to pour it.

After he had finished smoothing the concrete and placing his initials in it, he stood back with a big smile on his face. The neighbor's kids were chasing their dog that day and the dog ran through the concrete, and the children followed trying to apprehend the pet. There were footprints, and dog paw marks all in his beautifully finished concrete. When the old preacher saw this, he reached up and grabbed a rake and began chasing the dog and the children down the street.

After collecting himself he turned and started walking back home only to see his wife standing on the porch with her arms folded looking directly at him. She said to him in jest, "What is all this talk about Christian love for the past fifty years?" The old preacher said, "That was love in the abstract, this is love in the concrete."

Colossians 3:12 Put on therefore, as the elect of God, holy and beloved, bowels of mercies, kindness, humbleness of mind, meekness, longsuffering.

Lying Dog

A man saw a sign in yard which said, "Talking dog for sale," so he walked up and knocked on the door. When the owner answered, he asked, "Do you really have a talking dog?" "Sure do," the man replied. "Let me see him," the visitor requested. They walked around to the back yard and there lay a mutt by a dog house. The inquirer asked,

"Can you talk?" The dog said, "Yes, I can. I have been talking all my life." The astounded man said, "Wow, I guess you have amazed a lot of people?" The dog said, "No, not really, I don't let people know I can talk. It works to my advantage. I used to work as a spy because people didn't know that I could talk. They would say anything around me, so I gathered some valuable information. People will say anything around a dog because they think we can't talk. I've worked for the CIA, the FBI, and even with Special Forces in Afghanistan."

The man said, "Man, this is awesome. How much do you want for him?" "Five dollars." "Five dollars! Why are you selling a talking dog so cheap?" The owner looked at the visitor with disappointment on his face and said, "He's the biggest liar I've ever seen."

Colossians 3:9 Lie not one to another, seeing that ye have put off the old man with his deed.

Making Use Of Leftovers

My parents were culinary, fashion, and domestic geniuses. I've seen my mom eyeball two pairs of my jeans and decide which pair was more ragged. After making the determination, she would take the worst pair and cut them up and make patches for the best pair. I've seen her cut up blouses, dresses, and shirts, into small squares, and sew those squares together into blankets to throw over us while we slept at night. I have seen my mom fry chicken, and then take the grease from the chicken and put flour in it and make gravy for the rice.

We had to walk three quarters of a mile to the bus stop each cold winter morning, and often my sisters would complain about ashy legs. My mom took grease and rubbed their legs down and rubbed it on my face before we went out to the bus stop. My dad cut down maple trees, split those trees up into strips, and took those strips and made bottoms for chairs. The poor hog had no chance around our house. They threw virtually nothing away. I don't even remember us having a trash can.

Today, we deplore leftovers, but my mom knew how to make the best leftovers ever. The message of the miracle feeding of the 5000 is often overlooked. Our God always makes use of leftovers. He never wastes anything.

Mark 8:12 When I brake the five loaves among five thousand, how many baskets full of fragments took ye up? They say unto him, Twelve.

Man of the House

After reading a book entitled, "Man of the House," a young husband walked into his house pointed his finger into his wife's face, and said to her, "You're going to cook me one of the best dinners that you have ever prepared. It's going to begin with a fresh salad, and after that I want roast beef and mashed potatoes with all the trimmings. You will finish it off with strawberry shortcake for dessert. Then, you will go into the bathroom, and run me a tub of water at 112°. While I am bathing you will scrub my back, and when I get out of the tub my clothes will be neatly ironed and folded. When all of this is done, guess who is going to brush my hair and put on my shoes?" His wife responded, "Well I guess the undertaker."

1 Timothy 3:4 One that ruleth well his own house, having his children in subjection with all gravity.

Marriage and Money

A man married a very rich woman and she would not let him forget how much money she had. She told him," Joe you see that big Lincoln in the driveway? It wouldn't be here if it weren't for my money. You see that big boat in our back yard? It wouldn't be here if it weren't for my money. Look at this big house we live in. We wouldn't be in it if it weren't for my money." Joe couldn't take anymore so he told her, "Anna, the truth is I wouldn't even be here if it weren't for your money!"

Ecclesiastes 10:19 A feast is made for laughter, and wine maketh merry: but money answereth all things.

Me and My House

Years ago my son Cory had a cassette tape on his bed by "Red Head Kingpin." I had never heard of such a character, so I took the tape, put it in the cassette player, and listened to it. When I say that it was extremely vulgar and offensive, that is an understatement.

I took the tape, twisted it in two pieces and pulled it apart, and then laid it on his bed. I walked out and closed the door, knowing that he would see it when he came home from school. When he got home, I waited to see what his response would be. Sure enough, he came to me and said "Daddy, you been in my room!" I said to him, "Son, we got a problem; your room is in my house."

Ephesians 6:4 And, ye fathers, provoke not your children to wrath: but bring them up in the nurture and admonition of the Lord.

Me Worm

There was an old Indian who was converted to Christianity. He walked into a trading post and people began to make fun of him. They mocked him and said, "You say that you are a Christian. You don't even know what a Christian is. How are you saved?" The old Indian looked down on the ground and saw a worm. He took a match and lit a ring of fire around the worm. Just as the fire was about to engulf the worm, he reached down, pulled the worm out of the fire and said, "Me worm!" The hand of God pulls us out of the fire by His grace.

Romans 5:8 But God commendeth his love toward us, in that, while we were yet sinners, Christ died for us.

Meeting of Justice and Mercy

There is a story about the two major attributes of God, Justice and Mercy. One day, they planned a meeting down by Jacob's well at 12 o'clock. Justice showed up right on time as always, but mercy was nowhere to be found. Justice waited until one o'clock, but still mercy was nowhere to be found. At two, three and four o'clock, justice was still waiting, but mercy had not arrived.

Just about sundown, justice was about to leave the well and go home, but he looked down the road and saw mercy was coming over the horizon. When mercy walked up to justice he said, "I'm sorry I'm late, but I had to make a few stops. Justice said, "You look a mess. What happened to you?" Mercy said, "I was delayed, because I was needed in the Garden of Eden because Adam broke God's command and he would have been destroyed if I weren't there. I also had to rush to the aid of Moses because God told him to speak to the rock in the wilderness, but he struck it with his rod. I left there and went to the rescue of David, a man after God's own heart, but he committed adultery, and tried to cover it up with lies, and if I hadn't showed up on time he would have been destroyed forever. I also stopped by Calvary because there was a sinner whose name is a Ronnie Williams who continually makes mistakes. So, Justice, please excuse me for my lateness.

Mercy then turned and looked off in the distance and said to Justice, I'm sorry I got to go because ---- (fill in the blank with your name) needs me! We will talk later!

Titus 3:5 Not by works of righteousness which we have done, but according to his mercy he saved us, by the washing of regeneration, and renewing of the Holy Ghost;

Michael Jordan Didn't Quit

None of us know who Leroy Smith is or have ever seen him on a basketball court, but in the 1978-79 season at Laney Walker High School in Wilmington, N.C., he was chosen for the varsity team over Michael Jordan. Smith was 6'7 and Jordan was 5'10, according to the assistant coach Fred Lynch. Jordan didn't get angry; he didn't sulk but he settled for the junior varsity team where he became recognized as a promising player. His rejection for the varsity team only made him work harder on his game and the rest is history.

You may not have heard of Leroy Smith, but Michael Jordan is a household name because he is regarded as the greatest basketball player who ever graced the basketball court simply because he didn't give up. Some of us are on the verge of success, on the edge of victory, in plain view of a breakthrough, but we are getting ready to throw in the towel, raise the white flag of surrender and quit!

Ecclesiastes 9:11 I returned, and saw under the sun, that the race is not to the swift, nor the battle to the strong, neither yet bread to the wise, nor yet riches to men of understanding, nor yet favour to men of skill; but time and chance happeneth to them all.

Ministry Struggles

A little boy noticed that there was a cocoon on the ledge of his window with the moth struggling trying to get out. He decided that he would help the moth, so he went into the bathroom and got one of his father's razor blades. He carefully slit open the cocoon to help the month out and shortly thereafter it died. When his father came home the little boy asked him why the creature died. His father explained to him that the moth needed the struggle in order to live because struggling releases a hormone into the creature's body that's necessary for it to survive. The cutting edge of all our ministries is our struggles.

Job 23:10 But he knoweth the way that I take: when he hath tried me, I shall come forth as gold.

Mirrors Don't Lie

A man was walking down the street and he looked in a window and saw the ugliest man he had ever seen in his life. He thought to himself, "Look at those beady eyes with those bags under them. Look at that droopy face. He looks like he doesn't have a friend in the world. The way he's dressed, he must have gotten dressed in the dark. His shirt is dirty. His tie is twisted and he needs to wash his face." Then, it dawned on him that he was not looking through a window but a mirror.

James 1:22-24 22 But be ye doers of the word, and not hearers only, deceiving your own selves. For if any be a hearer of the word, and not a doer, he is like unto a man beholding his natural face in a glass: For He beholdeth himself, and goeth his way, and straightway forgetteth what manner of man he was.

My Father Said So

Two little boys were playing on the side of a hill one morning as the sun began to rise in the east. They played together all day without noticing the time. When the sun was about to set in the west, one little boy pointed towards the sun and said, "When we started playing this morning the sun was over there, but it has moved all the way over yonder." The second little fellow said "No, the sun didn't move at all, what happened was that the Earth moved around the sun and it appears the sun moved." The first boy said, "No, I saw it in the east this morning, but now it's in the west." The other boy said, "My father told me that the Earth revolves around the sun, while the sun never moves." "Well, you can believe what you want, but my eyes saw the sun move." The confident lad smiled and said, "So you can believe your eyes, but I choose to believe what my daddy said." Regardless of our circumstances, we should always believe what our father said rather than what we see.

I may be broke right now, but my father said the righteous has never been forsaken.

I may not have a job, but my father said He would supply all of my needs according to His riches in glory.

My friends may have walked away from me, but my father said He would never leave me nor forsake me.

My life may have been turned upside down, but my father said all things work together for my good.

My parents may be dead and gone, but my father said when mother and father forsake us, He will take us up.

My body may be in pain, but my father said with his stripes I'm healed.

I may have fallen into sin, but my father said He would forgive me for all unrighteousness.

I may die tonight, but my father said He has a mansion waiting on me in the heavens.

Numbers 23:19 God is not a man that he should lie; neither the son of man that he should repent: hath he said, and shall he not do it? Or hath he spoken, and shall he not make it good?

Nick at Night

I have a confession to make this morning. Sometimes it is difficult for me to sleep at night, so I sit up and watch television. Most times I will watch a news channel like MSNBC or CNN. Sometimes I watch the history channel to brush up on past events. Other times I try to see if I can find a good football or basketball game. One of the stations my remote usually ends up on is Nick at Night. A little "Sanford and Son," "Fresh Prince of Bel Air," "All in the Family," and "Everybody Loves Raymond" will sometimes do a brother good.

Nicodemus came to Jesus at night. Nicodemus was one of Jerusalem's most prominent citizens. He was a member of the Sanhedrin council which consisted of 71 men whose primary job was to address judicial concerns of the Jewish community. He was well respected and a venerated leader whose very appearance commanded respect. Can't you see him anxiously watching the clock waiting for the sun to go down? As the sun disappeared in the west and darkness settled over the streets of Jerusalem, he pulled his ball cap way down on his head. He flipped his coat collar up and slid his Ray-Bans on his eyes. He poked his head out of the door of his office and looked both ways to see if anyone was watching. He rapaciously meandered through the streets of Jerusalem not speaking to anyone in the hope that no one would recognize him.

He came to a little cottage in one of the villages where Jesus was and slowly entered the room. He broke the ice in a futile attempt to flatter Jesus by saying, "Rabbi, we know that thou art a teacher come from God; for no man can do these miracles that thou doest, except God be with him." Jesus side stepped his obsequious comment and got right to the issue at hand, by saying, "Verily, verily, I say unto thee, except a man be born again, he cannot see the kingdom of God." It would be these words that would cause all of Nicodemus' theology and studious assertions of the law to come collapsing down in a thunderous smoldering heap.

He came at night because he didn't want any of his colleagues to know that he was seeking the advice from a lowly carpenter, but he found out that night that this was no ordinary man. Jesus saved Nick that night, and his life was never the same again.

John 19:38-40 And after this Joseph of Arimathaea, being a disciple of Jesus, but secretly for fear of the Jews, besought Pilate that he might take away the body of Jesus: and Pilate gave him leave. He came, therefore, and took the body of Jesus. And there came also Nicodemus, which at the first came to Jesus by night, and brought a mixture of myrrh and aloes, about an hundred pound weight. Then took they the body of Jesus and wound it in linen clothes with the spices, as the manner of the Jews is to bury.

No Justice

A woman goes to have some pictures done and is asked to come back to proof them. When she comes in to see the pictures, she tells the photographer, "These pictures don't do me justice." The photographer retorted, "Lady you don't need justice, you need mercy."

Matthew 15:22 And, behold, a woman of Canaan came out of the same coasts, and cried unto him, saying, Have mercy on me, O Lord, thou son of David; my daughter is grievously vexed with a devil.

No Middle Man Needed

An old church mother went to the doctor and discovered that she had cancer. She went home and told her daughter what the doctor said and her daughter was distraught. Her daughter begged her to go to a local camp meeting that night so that the prophet could pray for her healing. The old Saint refused to go and her daughter wanted to know why. The old mother said, "Honey, I have already talked to the Lord about this, and it's in his hands. I know he can heal because he's healed me many times before, but if he doesn't heal me I still trust him. Besides, I've been talking to him for many years; I don't need a middleman now."

Hebrews 4:16 Let us therefore come boldly unto the throne of grace, that we may obtain mercy, and find grace to help in time of need.

No One Wants China Berries

A young pastor went to visit his mentor and said, "I have been lambasted by my congregation. My motives have been questioned. My integrity has been subverted, and my reputation has been soiled by pernicious attacks from people who listen to me preach every Sunday. These attacks have been proliferated by fellow ministers in my district, and I can't take it any longer. I'm ready to throw in the towel and quit, or I'm going to lay my religion aside and get some of them straight by confronting them about the lies they are telling. What advice can you give me?"

The wise old preacher walked over to the window and pulled back the curtain, and said "Son, what do you see out there?" The young man said, "I see two trees. There is a china berry tree and an apple tree." "What do you see in the apple tree?" asked the old preacher. "I see shoes, bike, tires, and other objects that people have been throwing at it to get the apples." "Do you see any objects in the china berry tree?" questioned the old sage. "No," was the youngster's answer. "Do you know why no one has been throwing objects at the china berry tree?" The old man continued. "No, why?" asked the young man. "It is because people don't want china berries," answered the old preacher.

There are people who are jealous of others because they want what they have. They want to live like they live. They want to do what they can do. They want to be who they are, but they can't. These people are jealous or envious, which is bad, but there is another group out there called haters. A hater hates because that's their nature. They can't help it. It's innate. It's instinctual. It's normal for them.

In their paper, "Attitudes, Without Objects," Justin Helper and Dolores Albarracin show that those who already held a lot of negative views are more likely to react negatively to new stimuli. In short, they discovered that some of the respondents acted negatively on any subject they presented, even if the subject was unrelated to anything that concerned them.

Proverbs 6:34 For jealousy is the rage of a man: therefore he will not spare in the day of vengeance.

Not Enough Rocks

In the movie, "Forest Gump," Forest and his girlfriend Jennie revisit the house where she grew up as a child. There were so many evil things that happened to Jennie that she walked up close to it and was overwhelmed with emotion because of so many bad memories. Then she picked up rocks and began to throw one rock right after another, until she succumbed to the ground in exhaustion. Forest slowly walked up and kneeled down besides Jennie and said, "Sometimes there just aren't enough rocks."

The lesson we can learn from Forest is that life can overwhelm us and throwing rocks is futile. If we would look back at our past and see all the hurt and agony that has been caused by others, it is impossible to cast rocks at each one of them. So, rather than throwing rocks, thank God that He kept you through it all.

1 Thessalonians 5:15 See that none render evil for evil unto any man; but ever follow that which is good, both among yourselves, and to all men.

Now Concerning the Collection

If I went to Kay's Jewelers and saw a watch that I liked, I would have to do three things to take it home with me. First, I would have to believe in my heart that I wanted the watch. But believing is not enough. Secondly, I would then have to walk over to the service representative and confess to him/her that I wanted the watch. Thirdly, if I believed and confessed that I wanted the watch, I would have to act out what I believed and confessed. That's exactly what happens when the clerk brings that watch and places it on the counter. She's actually saying, "Now concerning the collection?" It's not enough to say I'm saved, it must be proven at collection time.

1 Corinthians 16:1 Now concerning the collection for the saints, as I have given order to the churches of Galatia, even so do ye.

One Class at the Judgement

When the Titanic left Great Britain, there were three classes of people on it. There was the crew, first, second, and third class passengers. I'm told that they were sipping on champagne while the band was playing, and the dance floor was full of men and women enjoying themselves.

A distress call was sent out around 12 o'clock after they hit an iceberg, but there was no response. There were only 15 life boats on board with over 2000 passengers. The captain said, "Women and children first!" This distressed command prompted some men to dress up like women, so that they could get a place on a life boat. It was all futile for many of them because the Titanic slipped beneath the icy slick waters of the sea. When the ship went down, there were only two classes of people--the saved, and unsaved.

Matthew 25: 5-7 While the bridegroom tarried, they all slumbered and slept. And at midnight there was a cry made, Behold, the bridegroom cometh; go ye out to meet him. Then all those virgins arose, and trimmed their lamps.

Passed Redemption Point

A ship lost power on the Niagara River and was being towed by a tug boat when the rope snapped. There were many people on the crippled ship as it drifted slowly down river towards Niagara Falls. There is a point on the Niagara River called, "Passed Redemption

Point." When a vessel passes this point, there is no hope, because of the strong irresistible force of the current of the river. As the ship passed this point, all hope was lost for the passengers and crew.

Just as the ship came to the deep, foggy and ominous abyss of the deadly falls, the captain felt a strong wind hit his face. The captain shouted, "Raise the sails!" The men hoisted the sails and angled them up river and slowly the ship began to move up river and eventually went back past the "Passed the Point of Redemption." Soon the ship was in calm waters and headed up river. Somebody has drifted so far that you think that it is impossible to recover, but the captain is on board shouting to you to raise the sails!

Luke 23:42, 43 And he said unto Jesus, Lord, remember me when thou comest into thy kingdom. And Jesus said unto him, Verily I say unto thee, today shalt thou be with me in paradise.

Peace Is Better Than Closure

I was shopping in a clothing store in Atlanta when I heard a song on the intercom system called "Closure." I always see everything with sermonic eye, so I listened attentively as the young guy pleaded with his girlfriend to fornicate one more time so that he could receive closure. Just sleep with me one more time for closure, he begged. I thought to myself that his suggestion wouldn't do anything but create more problems.

There are some things we will never get closure about. My dad died in 2014, but I still get teary eyed sometimes when I think about him. My brother Eddie died in 1993, and the other day while talking to my son, I called him Eddie. We don't need closure; we need peace! I have peace with God because he lives!

John 14:27 Peace I leave with you, my peace I give unto you: not as the world giveth, give I unto you. Let not your heart be troubled, neither let it be afraid.

Perseverance of God

Because we are frail human beings and weak and sometimes inconsistent, unfocused, and ill equipped, we often start things, but leave them unfinished. How many of us have started a task and never finished? An unfinished backyard barbeque pit, an unfinished storage building, unfinished renovation of our home, a sweater we started knitting, a class we never completed, a degree we started, and the list goes on and on, all testify of our unwillingness or inability to stay on point and finish something we started.

We often overestimate the significance of just starting, but the reward does not come for just starting. No baseball team wins the pennant because they started the season, no football team wins the Super Bowl because they started pre-season; no horse wins the Purple Crown because he started the race; no boxer gets the belt because he starts sparring, and no one gets a gold watch because they start work. No one loses weight because they started dieting. No one gets a diploma because they started school. No one gets social security because they started work. No one grows into spiritual maturity because they started coming to church. No one prospers because they started tithing.

Often we throw up our hands too soon. We toss in the towel, bail out, jump ship, and go AWOL. In other words, we quit too soon and never finish I have good news. God finishes what He starts! He never quits.

Philippians 1:6 Being confident of this very thing, that he which hath begun a good work in you will perform it until the day of Jesus Christ:

Picking Up Bobby Pins When the World Is On Fire

A woman woke up one night and discovered her house was on fire. Her husband was lying next to her and her children were in the next room. The first thing she thought about was her beautiful hair, so she started grabbing bobby pins that she often used to keep up her hair. Her sons were in the next room about to die, but she was picking up pins. Her daughters were about to be engulfed in flames, but she was picking up pins. Her husband was inhaling toxic smoke, but this woman was more concerned about the insignificant things than the things that really mattered. The church cannot be guilty of picking up pins while this world is on fire.

John 12:25 He that loveth his life shall lose it; and he that hateth his life in this world shall keep it unto life eternal.

Pleasing My Master

A young man wanted to learn to play the violin, so he went out and bought an expensive instrument. He started taking classes from a master violinist, Antonio Stradivari. After years of training, he became a consummate violinist who travelled extensively across the globe. He decided to come back home and to do a concert in his home town. The arena was packed, both top and bottom with adoring fans. The young man began to play and people stood all around cheering to his beautiful music. The young man kept staring at the balcony and kept playing. The applause became louder and louder, but the young man kept making beautiful music. Finally, an old white-haired man stood up in the balcony and the violinist ceased playing. When asked why he had such a long performance, he responded, "My master was in the balcony and I couldn't stop until I pleased him."

Matthew 25:23 His lord said unto him, well done, good and faithful servant; thou hast been faithful over a few things, I will make thee ruler over many things: enter thou into the joy of thy lord.

Poor Workmanship

I worked as an apprentice carpenter years ago. One day, I was driving a nail into a piece of lumber and the nail bent. I kept nailing the crimped nail into the wood. My supervisor walked by and saw it and said to me, "That's poor workmanship. Don't ever do that because my name is at stake. You work for me and I don't want people to think that I am guilty of poor workmanship." He went on the say, "What you do is a reflection of my company. Make sure you cut the angles, drive nails cleanly, and clean up after you're done." He was concerned about his image as a carpenter. God is even more concerned about His image; therefore, He is never guilty of poor workmanship.

Ephesians 2:10 For we are his workmanship, created in Christ Jesus unto good works, which God hath before ordained that we should walk in them.

Portrait Of A Dead Church

A world renowned and celebrated artist, who was also a devout Christian, was attending Bible study one night. The pastor was teaching from the Book of the Revelation chapter 3 on the church of Sardis. The first verse says, "And unto the angel of the church in Sardis write, These things saith he that hath the seven Spirits of God, and the seven stars; I know thy works, that thou hast a name that thou livest, and art dead." Someone asked, "I wonder what does a dead church look like?" The pastor said, "Why don't we commission our brother here to paint us a picture of a dead church?" The artist agreed and immediately began painting his rendition of a dead church.

A few weeks later everyone was awaiting the unveiling of the portrait of a dead church. Many of the members of the church had gathered and had conjured up images in their minds as to what a dead church would look like. Some believed the painting would depict a church that was dilapidated with unkempt shrubbery, tall grass, and a broken cross on its steeple. Others thought the painting would show a small church with eight or ten old people sleeping while the minister was delivering his Sunday morning sermon. There were others who thought the portrait would portray four or five people in a huge sanctuary with no pastor in the pulpit.

But to their chagrin and dismay, when the artist unveiled his painting it was an exact replica of their church. Confusion broke out. Some of them erupted in disbelief and exclaimed, "We wanted you to paint a picture of a dead church!" The artist retorted, "We have no emphasis on evangelism. There is no missionary effort towards the poor in this community. We never do anything for this neighborhood, and the baptismal pool has cobwebs in it. This IS a dead church!"

Revelation 3:1 And unto the angel of the church in Sardis write; These things saith he that hath the seven Spirits of God, and the seven stars; I know thy works, that thou hast a name that thou livest, and art dead.

Power Of Touch

In 1944, an experiment was conducted on 40 newborn infants to determine whether individuals could thrive on basic physiological needs without affection. Twenty newborn infants were housed in a special facility where they had caregivers who would go in to feed them, bathe them, and change their diapers, but they would do nothing else. The caregivers had been instructed not to look at or touch the babies more than what was necessary, never communicating with them. All their physical needs were attended to scrupulously and the environment was kept sterile, so that none of the babies would become ill.

The experiment was halted after four months, by which time, at least half of the babies had died. At least two more died even after being rescued and brought into a more natural familial environment. There was no physiological cause for the babies' deaths. They were all physically very healthy. Before each baby died, there was a period where they would stop verbalizing and trying to engage with their caregivers. They stopped moving and would not cry or even change their expression. Death would follow shortly. The babies who had "given up" before being rescued died in the same manner even though they had been removed from the experimental.

Social scientists tell us that in order for a child to grow up emotionally stable they must have three things--acceptance, approval, and affirmation. The power of a touch can convey all three.

Matthew 8:14, 15 And when Jesus was come into Peter's house, he saw his wife's mother laid, and sick of a fever. And he touched her hand, and the fever left her: and she arose, and ministered unto them.

Praise the Lord

I've noticed that most churches have a praise team who are skilled at leading a congregation in praise and worship. Some churches spend a lot of money on musicians because it takes good music to get some people to praise the Lord. Some people need their favorite singer to get them there, but I would suggest that a sane person only needs a good memory to praise the Lord.

Psalms 146:1-5 Praise ye the Lord. Praise the Lord, O my soul. While I live will I praise the Lord: I will sing praises unto my God while I have any being. Put not your trust in princes, nor in the son of man, in whom there is no help. His breath goeth forth, he returneth to his earth; in that very day his thoughts perish. Happy is he that hath the God of Jacob for his help, whose hope is in the Lord his God:

Prayerful Fiancé

A young man went into a drugstore to buy three boxes of chocolate in small, medium, and large. When the pharmacist asked him about the three boxes, he said, "Well, I'm going over to my new girlfriend's house for supper. Then we are going out for the evening. If she only lets me hold her hand, then I'll give her the small box. If she lets me kiss her on the cheek, then I'll give her the medium box. But if she really lets me smooch seriously, I'll give her the large box."

He made his purchase and left. That evening as he sat down for dinner with his girlfriend's family, he asked if he could say the prayer before the meal. He began to pray, and he prayed a most earnest, and intense prayer that lasted for almost five minutes. When he finished his girlfriend said, "You never told me you were such a religious person." He said, "You never told me your dad was a pharmacist."

Matthew 26:41 Watch and pray, that ye enter not into temptation: the spirit indeed is willing, but the flesh is weak.

Praying for the Inside

A man was sitting in a congregation of believers with braces on his legs, and an alter call was extended. Sitting beside him was a cynic who had critiqued the whole service. The crippled man got up, grabbed his crutches, went to the altar, and prayed. The infidel sat and observed the whole process as everyone around the altar cried and invoked the presence of God.

When prayer time was over, the cripple picked up his crutches, hobbled back to his seat, and sat beside the critic. The unbeliever leaned over and said to the cripple, "You went up there crippled and came back crippled. If your God heard your prayer you would be walking like me." The cripple man responded, "You're looking at the outside, but if you could see the change on the inside, you would be amazed."

2 Corinthians 4:16 For which cause we faint not; but though our outward man perish, yet the inward man is renewed day by day.

Praying for Survival

There was a man who was shipwrecked on a small island. He built a little hut out on twigs and bamboo shoots and used a little candle to light it at night. Every day he would go down by the sea shore and watch for passing ships, and when he saw one he would scream to the top of his lungs, take off his tattered shirt, and wave it in the air to try and get their attention.

One day he saw a ship passing by, and per his custom, he tried to get the attention of the ship's crew. To his amazement he turned and saw his hut and everything he owned burning to the ground. As he lay on the ground weeping, he heard men approaching on a life boat.

He said to them, "I didn't think you noticed me." And they said, "A fire that big, how could we not see it?!" Sometimes The Lord will say no to a hut, but yes to survival! PRAY!

Luke 18:1 And he spake a parable unto them to this end, that men ought always to pray, and not to faint.

Praying in the Spirit

A while ago, I was visiting hospice of Greenwood to see one of my former deacons. As I was approaching my deacon's room, I saw a young man, who was also a preacher. He invited me to come in to pray for his pastor. I did not know the preacher, but the doctors had given him a short time to live. He was obviously in a lot of pain. It was difficult for him to breathe, and his languid eyes would only blink casually. I leaned over the bed, introduced myself, and he nodded because he didn't have enough strength to talk. As we were preparing to pray, another preacher friend of mine walked in the door who knew him.

We all joined hands around his bed, along with his family, and my preacher friend began to pray. I was so relieved because I did not want to pray. Don't get me wrong, I know the power of prayer and I believe in prayer, but the Holy Spirit was leading me to pray for his release. This was an elderly saint, who was in so much pain, and suffering, that the Holy Ghost was leading me to pray for his entry into heaven. We spend so much time praying to keep saints out of heaven, and too little time praying to get sinners into the Kingdom.

If we are led by the Holy Spirit, we must sometime pray some unpopular prayers. I'm not saying that we should go around praying for saints to die, what I am saying is that we must be so sensitive to the Holy Spirit, that he must direct us in how to pray. The Sweet Holy Spirit of God must prompt us in our prayers, prepare our prayers, and present our prayers. He prompts us because we don't know what to pray. Romans 8:26 "Likewise the spirit also helpeth our infirmities: for we know not what we should pray for as we ought." Secondly, He helps us because of our sinful nature; we don't know how to pray. Remember the disciples request to Jesus, "Lord teach us to pray." Thirdly; the Holy Spirit takes our prayers and presents them into the throne room of God.

Romans 8:26 ... "But the spirit itself makes it intercession for us with groanings which cannot be uttered."

Prideful Preacher

A young preacher proudly walked up into the pulpit one Sunday with his shoulders back, his chin up, with a slow swagger to his chair and sat down. When it came time for him to preach, he stood and nothing went right. He couldn't get his phrases straight; he slurred his words and kept repeating himself because he had forgotten scripture verses. He made an absolute mess. When he walked down off the stage, his head was down, and his body language reeked of embarrassment. An old lady sitting on the front seat said, "Young man, if you had gone up there the way you are coming down, you would have come down the way you went up."

1 Peter 5:5 Likewise, ye younger, submit yourselves unto the elder. Yea, all of you be subject one to another, and be clothed with humility:

for God resisteth the proud, and giveth grace to the humble.

Proper Posture for Prayer

Three preachers were debating about the correct posture in prayer. The first preacher said that the best way to pray is with your hands together with your head up towards heaven. The second preacher disagreed, and said the best posture in prayer is to bow on your knees and hold your head downward. The third preacher said, "Both of you are wrong. The correct posture in prayer is to lie down on the floor on your face prostrate before God."

There was a telephone repairman listening in on the conversation, so he could not help but overhear. He slowly walked to the preachers and said, "I don't mean any harm, but I think all of you are wrong." The preachers look at one another in amazement and one of them said, "You're just a telephone repair man, how would you know about praying?" The repairman said, "The best posture for prayer is when you're upside down on the telephone pole, suspended 40 feet in the air, with nothing holding you but telephone wires around your feet."

God often creates situations and circumstances that will put us in the correct posture for prayer.

You can't enjoy the stars without the night,

You can't be victorious in war without a fight,

You can't enjoy the sunshine without rain,

You can't be thankful for medicine without pain.

Exodus 14:10 And when Pharaoh drew nigh, the children of Israel lifted up their eyes, and, behold, the Egyptians marched after them; and they were sore afraid: and the children of Israel cried out to the Lord.

Pursuing Puppy

An old man was sitting on his porch one day and his little pup was playing in the front yard. There was a chain-linked fence around the old man's yard that he had installed to keep his little dog out of the street. His little dog ran up to the fence barking to the top of his voice at a huge bulldog, but he never broke his stride. The little dog continued barking and yelping at the bulldog because he was protected by the fence.

The bulldog turned the corner, never gave any attention to his yapping nemesis and walked out of sight. The old man got up from his rocker, went back into his house, fell down on his knees and prayed, "Lord give me some of that stuff that bulldog got."

Hebrews 12:2 Looking unto Jesus the author and finisher of our faith; who for the joy that was set before him endured the cross, despising the shame and is set down at the right hand of the throne of God.

Put Down Your Load

A man was riding down the road in his truck when he saw an old farmer carrying a sack of potatoes on his shoulders. He pulled over and asked the old guy if he wanted to ride into town. The old farmer got in the truck, but the driver noticed that the old farmer still had the sack of potatoes still on his shoulders. The driver asked, "Why don't you put down that heavy sack and lay it on the floor?" The old farmer said, "Sir I don't want to trouble you any further. You've already given me a ride. I wouldn't want you to be troubled with this sack of potatoes too." The driver said, "What trouble? If you're in my truck then so is the load you're carrying." If the Lord saved you, he can certainly carry your load.

1 Peter5:7 Casting all your care upon him for He careth for you.

140

Preacher Wants A Piece Of Chicken

A preacher was invited to preach at a homecoming service in a little town in South Georgia. As was their custom, they prepared a dinner before the service and the minister arrived early because he was famished.

He entered the line with his plate extended. As he approached an older lady who was serving the chicken, he said, "Give me a leg and a wing, please." The old lady took her fork and dropped a wing on his plate and turned to the next person in line. The minister was a little shocked because she only gave him one piece of chicken. He said to her, "Excuse me sister, but I asked for a leg also." She looked at him and said, "No!" Usually the preacher was unassuming and gentle in his speech, but he was hungry so he decided to throw his weight around. He responded, "Do you know who I am? I'm the guest speaker for the event!" The old lady never looked up when she said, "Do you know who I am? I'm the one with the chicken, and I was told to give one piece of chicken to everybody."

Ephesians 5:21 Submitting yourselves one to another in the fear of God.

Preaching Voice

Kenyatta Gilbert is a professor of homiletics at Howard University in Washington, DC. He is the author of "The Journey and Promise of African American Preaching." In his book he asserts that the African-American church is in dire condition because Black preachers have lost their voice. He believes that black preaching historically is what he calls "Trivocal Preaching." The black preacher has to have three voices-the prophetic voice, the sagely voice, and the priestly voice.

Sometimes a black preacher must preach prophetically, that is he has to accurately interpret the Scriptures so that people will understand clearly what God is saying in His Word. At other times a preacher must speak with the voice of a sage. This is paramount today because we have information at our finger tips, but no wisdom with the knowledge we've gleaned from the Internet. Lastly, the black preacher must speak with a priestly voice which he uses to bring Heaven and Earth together. He becomes an intermediary for God and mankind. I believe that Gilbert has a valid point because every preacher and Christian must discover his or her own voice.

I was talking to a young preacher just the other day and he asked me how I developed my preaching style. I explained it like this. "I tried to be so many people when I started preaching, one of whom was Bishop F.D. Washington. He was one of my favorite preachers. Then I tried to be like Apostle Johnnie Washington who pastored in New York City. Later on I began listening to Rev. Jasper Williams, who pastors in Atlanta Georgia. But I failed in my attempt to be them. One day, I don't know when it was, I became comfortable with Ronnie. And the rest is history.

1 Peter 4:10 As every man hath received the gift, even so minister the same one to another, as good stewards of the manifold grace of God.

Prince Doesn't Need Prayer

"Wait a few days before you waste any prayers." That was Prince's assurance to fans gathered for a dance party one night at his Paisley Park complex in Chanhassen, Minnesota after reports that he had suffered a health scare during a flight. Unfortunately, he died. The Prince of Peace told his disciples, "Watch and pray with me" in the Garden of Gethsemane. He went about a stone's throw away, fell on face, and prayed with such intensity that giant drops of blood oozed through his skin. He died also, but fortunately for us, he got up, and he is alive forever!

Matthew 26:41-42 Watch and pray, that ye enter not into temptation.

The spirit indeed is willing, but the flesh is weak. He went away again the second time and prayed, saying, O my Father, if this cup may not pass away from me, except I drink it, thy will be done.

Profit and Loss

A young man was feeling very proud of himself. As a brand-new college graduate he had taken the C.P.A. Exam and passed with flying colors. Now he was a full-fledged Certified Public Accountant. His father had been a farmer who had a little vegetable stand along the highway and owned his own business.

Filled with self-importance, the young man began to criticize his father's way of keeping books. He said, "Dad, you don't even know how much profit you've made. Over here in this drawer are your accounts receivable. Over there are your receipts. You keep all your money in the cash register. You don't have any idea how much you've made."

The father answered, "Son, when you were born I owned one pair of pants. Now, your brother is a doctor; your sister is an art teacher, and you are a C.P.A. Your mother and I own our home. We have a car and we own this little business. Now add that up, subtract the pants, and all the rest is profit."

Genesis 24:1 And Abraham was old, and well stricken in age: and the Lord had blessed Abraham in all things.

Problems, Problems

A man who had never flown before decided that he would conquer his fears and purchase a plane ticket. Being extremely nervous, he called his insurance company and added another hundred thousand dollars to his life insurance policy. On the day of the flight he paced back and forth in front of his terminal and noticed a Chinese restaurant and went in to get lunch. After eating, he grabbed a fortune cookie which read, "The investment purchase you just made will pay great dividends." This man had a problem.

Then there was an attorney who specialized in mal-practice law suits who won millions of dollars for his clients from the doctors who he had to call on for his operation. He, too, had a problem.

Matthew 6:34 Take therefore no thought for the morrow: for the morrow shall take thought for the things of itself. Sufficient unto the day is the evil thereof.

Procrastinating Frog

A boy told his father, "Dad, if three frogs were sitting on a limb that hung over a pond, and one frog decided to jump off into the pond, how many frogs would be left on the limb?" The dad replied, "Two." "No," the son replied. "There are three frogs and one decides to jump, how many are left?" The dad said, "Oh, I get it, if one decides to jump, the others would too. So there are none left." The boy said, "No dad, the answer is three. The frog only decided to jump." Does that sound like last year's resolution? We have good ideas and make great resolutions, but often times we only decide, and months later we are still on the same limb, doing nothing.

Exodus 8:9-10 And Moses said unto Pharaoh, Glory over me: when shall I entreat for thee, and for thy servants, and for thy people, to destroy the frogs from thee and thy houses that they may remain in the river only? And he said, tomorrow. And he said, be it according to thy word: that thou mayest know that there is none like unto the Lord our God.

Proof Needed

W.C. Fields was getting ready to travel abroad and he needed a passport. He went down to the Office of State and the agent asked for his birth certificate. Fields told her that he didn't have one and the lady said to him, "Sir you cannot acquire a passport from this office without proof of birth." Fields replied, "I'm here ain't I, what other proof you need?"

1 Kings 18:8 And he answered him, I am: go, tell thy lord, Behold, Elijah is here.

Providence Of God

Michelangelo was a Florentine sculptor, painter, architect, and poet of the High Renaissance who exerted an unparalleled influence on the development of Western art. Considered to be the greatest living artist during his lifetime, he has since been described as one of the greatest artists of all time.

The story is told that Michelangelo was asked how he created such a masterpiece of art like the statue of David. He responded by saying that he asked his workers to bring a large piece of marble from the quarries of Florence and place it in his studio. Then he took a hammer and chisel and removed everything from the mass of stone that didn't look like the image in his mind. The result is the celebrated statue of David.

As a matter of fact, God does all of us the same way. He fashions us. He chisels us. He shapes us. He configures us by using trials, tribulations, troubles, and hardships in order to remove everything from us that doesn't look like the vision He has in His mind.

Romans 8:29 For whom he did foreknow, he also did predestinate to be conformed to the image of his Son, that he might be the firstborn among many brethren.

Pruning His People

My grandfather had a pear tree in his front yard when I was a boy that would not bear pears. I remember one day he went out with a hand saw and cut off some the dead limbs and even hit it two or three time with an ax. That fall, the tree had so many pears on it that he had to prop it up with two by fours. Why did that happen?

A plant produces fruit when sap rises and travels throughout its limbs, and sometimes the sap can't get to the end of the limbs, because of dead branches which obstruct the path of the sap. A good gardener knows that he has to cut off dead branches to improve the plants productivity.

God does this through, troubles, hardships, and difficulties, mean people who hate us, cantankerous supervisors, and family problems. What destroys others will make a Christian stronger! That's the reason many of us don't look like what we been through.

John 15:2 Every branch in me that beareth not fruit he taketh away: and every branch that beareth fruit, he purgeth it, that it may bring forth more fruit.

Purpose

The vacuum cleaner has purpose; the lawn mower has purpose. The inventers of both saw a problem and created an invention to solve the problem. The lawn mower cannot vacuum a floor and the vacuum cleaner cannot cut grass. They both must be used according to what they were invented to do. Too many of us are trying to do something we were not created to do. Therefore, we are miserable because we are not fulfilling our purpose.

Acts 9:4-6 And he fell to the earth, and heard a voice saying unto him, Saul, Saul, why persecutest thou me? And he said, who art thou, Lord? And the Lord said, I am Jesus whom thou persecutest: it is hard for thee to kick against the pricks. And he trembling and astonished said, Lord, what wilt thou have me to do? And the Lord said unto him, Arise, and go into the city, and it shall be told thee what thou must do.

Reading Life's Odometer

I love my truck. I have 140,000 miles on the odometer, and with most of those miles there are memories. Some of those memories are happy ones, and some of them are not so happy. Some of those miles were put on my truck when I was filled with joy, and some were put on the odometer when I was in abject sadness.

Some of those miles were driven to my parents' house on Sunday evenings when I visited my mom and dad. Some miles were driven as I traveled to birthday parties, anniversaries, and graduations and some were driven as I witnessed the joy on the faces of loved ones who were filled with jubilation because of achievements and accomplishments of family members.

Some of those miles, however, were spent going to the hospital, the emergency room, CCI, and intensive care unit. I've put miles on my truck just to witness the agony, the misery, and the pain of some of the members of my church. Some of those miles were driven while going to vigils, funerals, and funeral homes to see the bloodstain eyes of hurting people who lost loved ones.

It behooves us to periodically stop and look at life's odometer. You will discover that life is filled with vicissitudes, ups and downs, trials, tribulations, bitter days, sweet days, good memories, bad memories, days of grief, days of happiness, and days of sadness. I'm sure the Apostle Paul didn't have a truck, car, or a chariot, but he's evaluating his journey and sharing his life's experiences with Timothy.

2 Timothy 4:6-7 For I am now ready to be offered, and the time of my departure is at hand. I have fought a good fight, I have finished my course, I have kept the faith:

Reading Someone Else's Mail

An atheist professor was standing in front of his class maligning the Bible. He said, "I have read the Bible from beginning to end, and it makes absolutely no sense to me." Then he became bold and asked, "How many of you in here believe that the Bible is the word of God?" One young Christian at the back of the room slowly raised his hand and said, "I believe that the Bible is God's love letter to the church." The professor said, "There are so many mistakes in the Bible. I cannot accept it as being relevant to today's culture, and I do not understand it." To this, the young Christian student said, "Sir, I mean no disrespect to you, but if you have read the Bible and makes no sense to you, it may be that you are reading someone else's mail."

2 Peter 1:21 For the prophecy came not in old time by the will of man: but holy men of God spake as they were moved by the Holy Ghost.

Read the Manual

I was driving and noticed that my 'low fuel' light had come on as a warning. I was on pins and needles and wondering how much farther I could go before my car would stop on the interstate. I thought for a moment, and then I looked in the glove compartment and grabbed the owner's manual. And after looking at the section labeled fuel gage, I discovered that I could drive at least 30 miles with the warning light on. I could relax and feel more comfortable until I got to the gas station because I had read the owner's manual.

The Bible is our owner's manual, and it tells us that we can have comfort because he knows exactly how far we can go before we're empty.

2 Timothy 3:16 All scripture is given by inspiration of God, and is profitable for doctrine, for reproof, for correction, for instruction in righteousness:

Real Faith

Faith is not taking a flying leap in the dark. Faith is standing on the promises of God.

Faith is not believing in spite of evidence. Faith is obeying in spite of consequence.

Faith is not just believing God for what you want. Faith is receiving from God what he gives.

Faith, like film, is developed in the dark.

Hebrews 11:1 Now faith is the substance of things hoped for, the evidence of things not seen.

Real Sacrifice

A pig, chicken, and a cow were talking about what they gave the farmer. The cow said "Well, I give cream, and butter, and milk." The chicken said, "I give eggs that he can boil, fry sunny side up, over easy, or over well. The pig said, "I give bacon, ham, and pork chops. The difference is y'all give a donation. When I give, that's the end of me!"
Romans 12:1 I beseech you therefore, brethren, by the mercies of God, that ye present your bodies a living sacrifice, holy, acceptable unto God, which is your reasonable service.

Rejected Stone

Tradition has it that when they were building Solomon's Temple, they cut each stone at the bottom of the Mountain of Zion, and then brought the stones into the Temple to set them in place. The cornerstone was prepared at the bottom of the hill, and they brought it to the workers in the temple, but the workers overlooked the cornerstone and paid little attention. The stone lay there for many months, and finally grass grew over it and it rolled down the hill.

When the builders got ready for the cornerstone, which was necessary for the completion of the building, they sent word down to the quarry, "Send us the cornerstone!" They received this response, "We've already sent it up to you!" There was a frantic search for the stone and they finally found it at the bottom of the hill, and with much labor they brought it and set it in place. The builders rejected the stone, but ultimately had to go back, and get it to complete the building.

Jesus, like the rejected cornerstone, came to his own people and was despised and rejected. And so will we, as Christians, be rejected. Before it's all over, the world will have to give recognition to the church as the cornerstone.

Mark 12:9-11 What shall therefore the lord of the vineyard do? He will come and destroy the husbandmen, and will give the vineyard unto others. And have ye not read this scripture; the stone which the builders rejected is become the head of the corner: This was the Lord's doing, and it is marvelous in our eyes?

Remember Me

Everyone wants to be remembered. The architect of a building puts his name at the bottom of the blueprint because he wants everyone to remember he designed it. The contractor who builds the building places a sign in front of the building, so that we will remember who built it. Mothers save locks of hair and baby shoes because they want to remember when the baby was an infant. The person who created your suit or dress put a label in the collar because he wants everyone to remember who made that garment. Every automobile has a logo on it because the automaker wants us to remember who made it. We name our children Junior, and we give them our last name because we want them to remember their family. If we want to be remembered, it stands to reason that God should also be remembered.

Jesus took his disciples into the upper room and there he broke bread, ate the Last Supper and drank wine and gave it to his disciples and said to them, "As often as you do this, do it in remembrance of me."

1 Corinthians 11:24 And when he had given thanks, he brake it, and said, Take, eat: this is my body, which is broken for you: this do in remembrance of me.

Restoration Of the Backslider

An eagle with a broken wing. A race horse with a broken leg. A muscle car with no engine. A lion with no teeth. A rose with no fragrance. A harp with no stings. A church with no power, all these are bad sights. But a backslider is sadder still. One of the most pitiful pictures on Earth is that of a backslider. What is a backslider?

A backslider is one who slides back. God created us to be prosperous, to be producers, givers, full of joy and peace. And we are given all of these when we become Christians. But when we backslide, we willfully slide back from all that God has given us as our inheritance as a child of God. I was taught in the old Church that when a person backslides they forfeit their right as a Christian. The old saints taught us that when a person backslides, they are on their way to hell. They believed that a Believer could lose his salvation and become unsaved, and if they repented, they had to be saved all over again. The most miserable person in the world is not the overt sinner, but the unhappiest person you will ever meet is a backslider. If this is you today, I have some good news, you can be restored.

Psalms 51: 10 Create in me a clean heart, O God; and renew a right spirit within me.

Resurrected Flesh

I said my prayers last night before I went to bed trying to crucify the flesh. As believers we must die daily. So my prayer last night, tonight, and tomorrow night, and every night will be, "God help me with me." But every morning I get up flesh is sitting right by my bed side waiting on me. That's what Paul was talking about when he said, "In my flesh there was no good thing."

omans 7:18 For I know that in me (that is, in my flesh,) dwelleth no good thing: for to will is present with me; but how to perform that which is good I find not.

Rewards In Heaven

Joseph Francis Macaluso, nicknamed Joe Mac was born on April 21, 1973 in Stanton Island NY. He currently lives in Burbank California. His profession is key grip. He supervises the camera crew. He makes sure that all of the people filming a movie are doing their job correctly.

You have never heard of Joe Mack, but if you have seen the movie "Black Panther," you've seen his work. He was the key grip in that movie. I know you've heard of Chad Boseman who was the star, but you paid no attention to Joe Mac. If you sat through the movie to watch the credits, Joe Mack's name appeared on the same screen as Chad Boseman's.

You don't have to be a star to be in God's show. You can be a key grip, overlooked by people, standing at the door of the church, picking up paper on the church campus, cutting grass in the cemetery, driving a van, or changing diapers in the nursery. When the roll is called up in heaven, God will call your name.

Revelation 20:12 And I saw the dead, small and great, stand before God; and the books were opened: and another book was opened, which is the book of life: and the dead were judged out of those things which were written in the books, according to their works.

Rich Father

Two boys were walking along one day, one was rich and the other was poor. As they walked, the rich kid boasted about what his father owned. They saw a yacht sailing on the sea and the rich kid said, "You see that J. K. Rowling's luxury yacht sailing over there? It belongs to my father." They continued walking and the rich boy saw a plane flying overhead. The rich kid said, "You see that Eclipse 550 Twin Engine Executive jet flying there. It belongs to my father." As they kept walking, they saw a huge mansion on a hill and again the rich kid said, "You see that mansion on that hill. It belongs to my father." The poor kid couldn't take it any longer.

He grabbed the rich kid by the hand and began walking in the opposite direction and said, "You see that hill that your father's house is built on? It belongs to my father. The air that your father's plane is flying in belongs to my father also. The water that your dad's ship is sailing on belongs to my father. So see I'm a Christian and Heaven and Earth and all that is in them belongs to my Father.

Psalms 24:1 The Earth is the Lord's, and the fulness thereof; the world, and they that dwell therein.

Role Model

A young mother was attempting to do her house work one day as her little daughter constantly walked behind her with every step she took. The mother couldn't move unless she bumped into her daughter, so she suggested that she go watch television. The little girl said, "No mom, I'd rather follow you around the kitchen." As the mother headed towards the wash room, the little girl followed with a big smile on her face. The mom bent over to pick up clothes off the floor and turned to put them in the washer. As she turned, she stepped on the little girl's foot. The little girl started to cry, and the mother shouted, "I told you to go watch TV!" But the cute little girl looked up at her mom with huge drops of tears falling from her big brown eyes and said, "The Sunday School teacher told us Sunday to walk in Jesus footsteps, but I can't see him, I only see you."

Titus 2:3-5 The aged women likewise, that they be in behaviour as becometh holiness, not false accusers, not given to much wine, teachers of good things; That they may teach the young women to be sober, to love their husbands, to love their children, To be discreet, chaste, keepers at home, good, obedient to their own husbands, that the word of God be not blasphemed.

Run Wilma

Wilma didn't get much of a head start in life. A bout with polio left her left leg crooked and her foot twisted inward, so she had to wear leg braces. After seven years of painful therapy, she could walk without her braces. At age 12, Wilma tried out for a girls' basketball team, but she didn't make it. She was undeterred, so she practiced with her friends every day. The next year she made the team.

When a college track coach saw her during a game, he talked her into letting him train her as a runner. By age 14 she had outrun the fastest sprinters in the U.S. In 1956 Wilma made the U.S. Olympic team, but showed up poorly. That bitter disappointment motivated her to work harder for the 1960 Olympics in Rome--and there Wilma Rudolph won three gold medals, the most a woman had ever won. We can't quit because it's just too soon to quit. We can't quit because Jesus didn't quit on us; therefore, we can't quit on him.

1 Corinthians 9:6 I therefore so run, not as uncertainly; so fight I, not as one that beateth the air.

Sanford and Son

The situation comedy "Sanford and Son" appeared on national TV in the 70s. Many of us remember Fred and Lamont along with Aunt Ethel, Bubba, Rollo, even Skillet and Leroy. This show is still in syndication today because people are still enjoying the antics of Fred Sanford the junk man who lived in the poor section of Watts, California.

When you boil down the show to its bare essence and look at the plot of each show, it was simply this: A father sends his son out to collect junk to bring it back for restoration. That's what God did with his Son.

John 3:16 For God so loved the world, that he gave his only begotten Son, that whosoever believeth in him should not perish, but have everlasting life.

Satan's Garage Sale

There is a legend about Satan having a garage sale. He had a table out front with lies on it, lust, temptation, bigotry, racism, and hated all stacked on the table. But over in the back behind some boxes, was discouragement. Someone asked why he had discouragement off the table he said that it was not for sale. His response was, "I will never get rid of discouragement because it is the most effective weapon I have against faith, it worked on Abraham in Egypt, when he lied about Sarah not being his wife. It worked in Moses in the wilderness, it worked on Jeremiah in prison, it worked on John the Baptist, and it even worked of Jesus in the Garden of Eden"

Ephesians 6:11 Put on the whole armour of God, that ye may be able to stand against the wiles of the devil.

Satan Hates Babies

From 1987 to 1990 Al and Peg Bundy propelled themselves to the top of the Nielsen ratings in the sitcom "Married with Children." Most of us watched it to see if Al could top the most ridiculous thing he'd said on the previous week and usually he did. They poked fun at the institution of marriage and rearing children and made a mockery of the family unit. This is how the world wants us to see the institution of marriage and raising children. The reason is that the world, the flesh, and the devil hate babies. Why? We have to remember that there are three basic reasons for the institution of marriage. First, the marriage institution models Christ's relationship with his church. Jesus is called the Bridegroom and the church is called the Bride of Christ who gives birth to born-again believers.

Secondly, there is the companionship component. Adam and Eve, who made up the first family, were to complement, co-operate, and communicate with each other. Satan hates the idea of harmony in the home. Thirdly; and more importantly, the family was created to produce babies. Genesis 1:28 "And God blessed them, and God said unto them, be fruitful, and multiply, and replenish the earth, and subdue it and have dominion over the fish of the sea and the final of the air and every living thing that moves upon the earth." The keyword is replenish.

We see an all-out attack against children and babies throughout the Scriptures. There was an attack on babies in the time of Moses when Pharaoh destroyed all of the male children to reduce the population of Hebrews. Also, at the time of Jesus it was Herod who ordered the murder all of the male children under age two to try to destroy Jesus. As F.W Boreham says, "When God sees that in this poor old world, a wrong needs righting or a truth needs preaching or a benefit needs inventing! He sends a baby." That's why today's youth are under attack.

Matthew 2:16 Then Herod, when he saw that he was mocked of the wise men, was exceeding wroth, and sent forth, and slew all the children that were in Bethlehem, and in all the coasts thereof, from two years old and under, according to the time which he had diligently inquired of the wise men.

Seeing Jesus In the Dark

Gardner Taylor pastored the 14,000-member Concord Baptist Church of Christ in New York City for over 40 years, but he started as a young preacher in Baton Rouge, Louisiana. It was during the darkest days of the Great Depression, and young Taylor was in the middle of a sermon one Sunday night. Suddenly the electricity in the small church went out. Standing there in the darkness, Taylor stood motionless. He didn't know what to do, but finally, an older deacon yelled out from the congregation, "Preach on, preacher! We can still see Jesus in the dark."

John 1:5 And the light shineth in darkness; and the darkness comprehended it not.

Setting Limits

A wealthy Texas rancher traveled to Africa for a hunting expedition and came across a wealthy African landowner who had no fences around his property. The Texan was confused, so he asked the African why was it that there was no fences around his property. He said to him, "Back home we always erect fences because they contain and restrict our animals from exceeding boundaries and it also marks our property lines." The African magnate said, "Sir, in this country, fences aren't needed because boundaries aren't fixed, besides whenever you put up fences, you always fence out more land than you fence in and I'm not finished acquiring land yet."

Boundaries and limits can be both useful and beneficial, but they can also be disadvantageous and even harmful. If you travel back towards Anderson on Hwy 29 at some point you will come to a sign, which reads, "Anderson city limits." That sign is there to let you know you're out of the jurisdiction of the county government and in the jurisdiction of the city government. If you take Hwy 29 south, at some point you will come to a sign which says, "Entering the State of Georgia." That sign marks the boundary of the state of Georgia. The sign denotes the fact that you are under the jurisdiction of the state of Georgia.

Limits also are helpful in mathematics. Calculus hinges on limits. As a matter of fact, math itself is useless without limits. Limits in math define continuity, derivatives, and integrals.

Many of us have limits as to how far we will go with people. Have you ever had someone who continually came to you to borrow money or your personal belongings and never brought them back? Limits are necessary in homemaking. Every household ought to have a budget. Do you have a budget at your house? If not, you're asking for trouble. Establish limits in your life, and resolve never to cross them.

When it comes to obeying God and trusting His Word, take the limits off. God wants us to live our lives in Him without putting limits on our faith. Israel limited God and wondered in the wilderness for 40 years, and many died without inheriting the Promised Land.

Psalms 78:41 Yea, they turned back and tempted God, and limited the Holy One of Israel.

Sick Deacon

A pastor took a church that had a reputation of being controlled by the deacons, particularly the deacon's chairman. Everything this pastor presented was shot down by this overbearing and headstrong leader of the board of deacons. If the young pastor suggested changes, the deacon was against it. If the pastor brought suggestions of how the church could benefit from acquiring adjacent properties of the church, this man was against it. It seems that everything this pastor proposed was opposed by the mean-spirited.

The deacon became gravely ill and was lying on his death bed in the hospital. He sent for his pastor to come and pray for him. The pastor showed up and prayed the most sincere, stirring and moving prayer over this man and noticed that he was had a tear falling from his eye. The pastor said, "What wrong deacon?" The miserly deacon said, "Bruh pastor, thank you for praying for me. I really appreciate you coming here today praying for me. If I die, I want you to know I'm sorry for all I've done to you." The pastor started to walk away when the deacon said to him, "Bruh pastor if I live, everything is just like it was."

Matthew 5:22-24 But I say unto you, That whosoever is angry with his brother without a cause shall be in danger of the judgment: and whosoever shall say to his brother, Raca, shall be in danger of the council: but whosoever shall say, Thou fool, shall be in danger of hell fire. Therefore if thou bring thy gift to the altar, and there rememberest that thy brother hath ought against thee; Leave there thy gift before the altar, and go thy way; first be reconciled to thy brother, and then come and offer thy gift.

Silver Spoon

I don't think many of us were born with a silver spoon in our mouth. The term "silver spoon" originated in Medieval England when people used wooden spoons to eat. It was possible to lacerate or stick a splinter in one's mouth or tongue from a worn spoon. This was not so with the wealthy aristocracy, who used silver spoons when eating. It was a tradition in many countries for wealthy godparents to give their godchildren a silver spoon at christening ceremonies, hence the term "born with a silver spoon in one's mouth."

Most of us, if not all of us, were born poor. Most of us know how to survive with the basics of life. We are accustomed to making ends meet and living from paycheck to paycheck. We had two meal choices in most of our homes when we were kids, "Take it or leave it." But I've learned that the fellow who has no money is poor, but the fellow who has nothing but money is much poorer.

Revelation 3:16-17 Because thou sayest, I am rich, and increased with goods, and have need of nothing; and knowest not that thou art wretched, and miserable, and poor, and blind, and naked: I counsel thee to buy of me gold tried in the fire, that thou mayest be rich; and white raiment, that thou mayest be clothed, and that the shame of thy nakedness do not appear; and anoint thine eyes with eye salve, that thou mayest see.

Sin

I asked God why some people aren't transformed by the Word. All Christians know that the Word will change our lives, but it seems to have no effect on some people. Even though they come to church incessantly, they remain the same. God spoke this to me, "They are not convinced of their sin." I pondered those words for a while and it dawned on me what God was saying. Until we see our wretchedness and how vile sin is before God, we will think that we are just fine. God help us to see us and not others. Isaiah 6:1-8 "Then said I, Woe is me!" The Apostle Paul declared, "O wretched man that I am!" If we never see that we have a problem of sin, there will never be a promotion to spiritual maturity.

Romans 7:24 O wretched man that I am! Who shall deliver me from the body of this death?

Sin Of Unbelief

A man went to his pastor and said, "I'm so miserable, I have been unfaithful to my wife, and I can't sleep at night, I have night sweats and nightmares, and I don't know what to do." The wise pastor says, "Son asked the Lord to forgive you and move on." The young man said, "I've done that every night since it happened, but I'm still feeling this sense of guilt for my adultery." The pastor then says to him, "Brother your problem is not adultery, its unbelief."

1 John 1:9 If we confess our sins, he is faithful and just to forgive us our sins, and to cleanse us from all unrighteousness.

Singing In a Storm

An ancient King wanted to decorate his throne room with a painting that would describe peace and tranquility. He discovered that he had three artists in his domain and he called them before him. Then he commanded them to go forth and create a painting that described peace and tranquility.

Months later, the artists were brought back to the presence of the king with their creations. The first artist brought a painting of a golden sunset over an azure blue sea with scintillating rays ricocheting off the surface of the water. The king said, "That's good." Then he called in the second painter. He brought a picture of a waterfall falling from jagged rocks. The landscape around the waterfall was laced with beautiful flowers, roses, carnations and lilies. The king said, "That's good." The last painter came in front of the king and he brought a painting depicting a tumultuous storm. The wind whipped the trees until they bowed low. The torrential rain fell heavily in the background, but in the center of the picture was a bird's nest where a little bird was looking up toward heaven singing. The king shouted, "That's the one! In the midst of a storm that little bird has peace and tranquility."

Like the little bird, Christians can sing in the midst of a storm because we have the assurance that the Lord is always present in our lives.

Acts 16:25 And at midnight Paul and Silas prayed, and sang praises unto God: and the prisoners heard them.

Smoking John 3:16

A missionary went deep into the heart of Africa to win souls for Christ. There is a fundamental tactic that's used by all missionaries, and that's to win the tribal leader first. If the leader of the tribe can be won to Christ, then the rest of the tribe will most likely follow suit.

This missionary went to a village and began to witness to a pagan king. He explained to him that if he would receive Jesus Christ as Lord, his life would be radically changed. He handed this old tribal leader a New Testament Bible. The pagan king took the Bible from the missionary, looked at it for a minute, then he tore a page out of it. He poured tobacco on the page, rolled it up, and lit it, and began to smoke it. The missionary said to him, "Sir, I want you to do one thing for me before you smoke another page. Please read it before you smoke it."

The missionary left the African village, and he returned five years later. As he approached the village, he saw a church that was packed to its capacity. He walked in and was surprised to see the old tribal leader preaching the gospel of Christ.

After the service he asked the old king what happened. The King said, "After you left, I begin to smoke the Bible. I smoked Matthew, Mark, and Luke. I smoked the first and second chapter of John, but when I got to the third chapter, and started reading about Nicodemus, I saw myself. And when I got to the 16th verse of the third chapter the Holy Ghost got a hold of me. I looked at my hands and they looked new. I looked at my feet and they did too.

John 3:16 For God so loved the world that he gave his only begotten Son, that whosoever believeth in him should not perish, but have everlasting life.

Snake Handlers Meeting

A man went to a church where they handle snakes in the service. It was all right with him as long as the preacher was handling the snakes, but then they brought more snakes in and threw them on the floor. The guy looked at the person next to him and asked, "Where is the back door?" His friend said, "There is no back door." The fellow said, "Well, you're getting ready to have one."

Deuteronomy 6:16 Ye shall not tempt the Lord your God, as ye tempted him in Massah.

Some Things Money Can't Buy

Money can buy a house, but money cannot buy a home. Money can buy food, but money cannot buy an appetite. Money can buy a wedding, but money cannot buy a marriage. Money can buy medicine, but money cannot buy health and strength. Money can pay tuition and buy books but money cannot keep you from being a fool. Money can buy churches, stain glass windows, and carpeted floors, but money cannot buy salvation. I'm glad that money can't buy salvation because if money could buy grace, the rich would live and the poor would die.

Acts 8:20 But Peter said unto him, Thy money perish with thee because thou hast thought that the gift of God may be purchased with money.

Son Will Let You In

A Union soldier received word that his mother was gravely ill back home and he needed to get home as quickly as possible. He went to his commanding officer and requested leave to go home before his mom passed. His platoon leader told him that he didn't have the authority to make that decision, so he had to go to a higher ranking officer and make his appeal.

The soldier decided that he would go directly to President Abraham Lincoln and ask for a furlough, but when he got there, two guards told him that he could not get in to see the president. He sat down on the White House steps and wept.

A little boy came by and saw him and asked why he was crying. He told the lad that his mother was dying back home and he needed to go home right away to see her, but he couldn't get in to see the president. The little boy grabbed the soldier by the hand and said, "Follow me." When they got to the same two soldiers who denied him entrance, they gave way and let them walk right through. They came to the Oval office and there were two other guards standing there, but when they came up to them, they too, gave them passage. The little fellow walked right up to the president and said, "Daddy, this man needs to see you."

There are some who wrongly believe that there are many ways to God. Others claim that Allah is the way, some say Buddha is the way, many believe that one must espouse to their religious doctrine, join their church, be baptized in their pool by their pastor, some claim that people must perform certain feats, but there is only one way to God, that is through His Son Jesus Christ.

John 14:6 Jesus saith unto him, I am the way, the truth, and the life: no man cometh unto the Father, but by me.

Source of Strength

A missionary in Africa lived in his central mission that had a small generator to supply current for the church and a small parsonage. Some natives from an outlying mission came to visit the pastor. They noticed the electric light hanging from the ceiling of his living room. They watched wide-eyed as he turned the little switch and the light went on. One of the visitors asked if he could have one of the bulbs. The missionary, thinking he wanted it for a sort of trinket, gave him one of the extra bulbs.

On his next visit to the outlying mission, the preacher stopped at the hut of the man who had asked for the bulb. Imagine his surprise when he saw the bulb hanging from an ordinary string. He explained that one needed to have electricity and a wire to bring the current to the bulb. The native had the mistaken notion that the bulb lit itself, not realizing the source of its power came from the generator. We are just trinkets, but God is our source.

Philippians 2:15 That ye may be blameless and harmless, the sons of God, without rebuke, in the midst of a crooked and perverse nation, among whom ye shine as lights in the world.

Spider's Web

Frederick Nolan was fleeing from his enemies during a time of persecution in North Africa. Being pursued by them over hill and valley with no place to hide, he fell exhausted into a cave, expecting his enemies to find him soon. Awaiting his death, he saw a spider weaving a web.

Within minutes, the little bug had woven a beautiful web across the mouth of the cave. When the hostile natives arrived they wondered if Nolan was hiding there, but only seeing the unbroken and unmingled piece of art, they thought it impossible for him to have entered the cave without dismantling the web, so they went on their way. Having escaped, Nolan later wrote in his memoirs, "Where God is, a spider's web is like a wall. Where God is not, a wall is like a spider's web."

Psalms 27:5 For in the time of trouble he shall hide me in his pavilion: in the secret of his tabernacle shall he hide me; he shall set me up upon a rock.

Spiritual Glaucoma

My dad had glaucoma which eventually robbed him of his sight.

He died blind, but praise God he can see now. Without boring you with the medical jargon, simply put, glaucoma is the gradual build-up of fluid in the eye which causes pressure on the optic nerve. As the pressure continues over a long period of time, a person will become blind. It's been called "The Sneaky Thief of Vision." Just as high blood pressure has been nicknamed the "Silent Killer," glaucoma is the silent blinder.

According to The World Health organization, glaucoma is the second leading cause of blindness in the world, next only to age related macular degeneration. Even though my dad was blind, he still had vision. One of the most moving moments of my life was watching him bow and pray over his food, even though he had to eat with his hands because he couldn't see the food he was eating. The sad truth today is that many Christians have spiritual glaucoma. They eat food threes time a day and never thank the God who provided it.

Colossians 4:2 Continue in prayer, and watch in the same with thanksgiving.

Spiritual vs Physical

I saw a bumper sticker which read, "We are spiritual beings having a physical experience." There are things we can learn from bumper stickers. I don't know if the driver was a Christian, but this is an accurate biblical principal. We have heard this statement in reverse. We usually hear it like this, "We are physical beings having spiritual experience." The truth is that this is the way the world perceives life. Most people spend all of their time ministering and accommodating the flesh and completely overlook the spiritual part of their lives.

Did you know that Americans, in 2014, spent 8 billion on cosmetics? They also spent 12 billion on cosmetic surgery. Also, 538 billion dollars were spent on clothes. That's $1700 per household. Americans also spent 20 billion dollars at the beauty salon. U.S. News and World Report estimated an average price for a haircut for women in New York is $73. In Minnesota, a woman's haircut costs $41 and $31 for men. In San Francisco a haircut for a man costs $49. In 2008 the economy tanked because of the collapse of the auto and housing industry. We love cars, clothes, cash, and creature comforts.

Nick Berry is the president of Data Genetics and was trained as a rocket scientist and air craft designer. In his blog, Berry analyzed the human body that weighed 176 lbs. A body that weighs 176lbs. is 61% water. If you look at the chemical makeup of the human body in terms of dollars and cents it would look like this. The oxygen would be worth $9.63, Carbon $.0.18, hydrogen, $1.60, nitrogen $0.18, calcium $0.11, phosphorus $0.89, potassium $104.00, sulfur $0.02, Chlorine $0.11, and magnesium $0.07. Total cost of the human body is $160.00. Why is it that we put more emphasis on a temporal body that's worth $160 and neglect the spirit that's eternal?

Dr. J.W. Wright, who pastored the Bethlehem church once said, "We walk around with a twenty-dollar hat on a ten cent head. The late A. Louis Patterson put it like this, "It doesn't matter how much your car is worth. You will have to park it. It doesn't matter how much your suit costs, you have to hang it up. And it doesn't matter how large your TV screen is, you got to turn it off." The Bible tells us that the spirit of man is far more important than the body.

2 Corinthian 5: 1 For we know that if our earthly house of this tabernacle were dissolved, we have a building of God, an house not made with hands, eternal in the heavens.

Standing in the Lord's Shoes

An old woman was being teased by an atheist. He said, "Emma I hear you're a saint now." She said, "I don't know about that but I'm saved." He asked, "What does that mean?" The old mother said, "It means that I'm standing in the Lord's shoes and he's standing in mine."

Galatians 2:20 I am crucified with Christ: nevertheless I live; yet not I, but Christ liveth in me: and the life which I now live in the flesh I live by the faith of the Son of God, who loved me, and gave himself for me.

Stay Focused

An old hunter went shopping for a hunting dog, and when he found one, he was assured the one he purchased was the best in the state. He took this dog out in the woods and immediately, the dog picked up the scent of a bear. The old hunter was excited, but a deer crossed the tracks of the bear, and the dog followed the tracks of the deer.

After following the tracks of the deer for a while, the dog picked the scent of a rabbit that had crossed the tracks of the deer. The dog followed the tracks of the rabbit for several yards, and then picked up the scent of a field rat, so he left the rabbit's trail and ended up barking down the hole of a polecat.

The problem in life for most of us is that we are not focused on the main goal of life. If you were asked what consumes you, drives you, motivates you, or makes your life worth living, what would you say? What is your main thing? What is the one thing that you live for? If you say anything other than worship, you are unhappy. No one is happy who does not put worship first. God created us to worship Him.

Jesus reminded a rich young ruler of this fact in the gospel of Mark. This young man had health because the scripture said that he came running. He also had wealth because the Bible said that he was a rich. He had energy and enthusiasm because he was young. And not only that, but he was also a well-respected man in the community because the Bible says that he was a ruler. However, there was one issue. *"Then Jesus beholding him loved him, and said unto him, One thing thou lackest: go thy way, sell whatsoever thou hast, and give to the poor, and thou shalt have treasure in heaven: and come, take up the cross, and follow me."* Mark 10:17-27.

On another occasion Jesus paid a visit to the small home of Martha, Mary and Lazarus. Mary sat at the feet of Jesus as Martha frantically worked in the kitchen. When Martha appeared in the doorway, she asked Jesus to tell Mary to help her. Jesus rebuked Martha and commended Mary for her persistence in worship.

Luke 10:42 But one thing is needful: and Mary hath chosen that good part, which shall not be taken away from her."

Still Dead

I loved cowboy shows when I was a kid, and I noticed that when they buried a dead man they lowered him down in a hole with ropes tied to a wooden box. It is nothing like that today.

When you die today, your body is taken to a mansion with manicured lawns, trimmed hedges, and beautifully decorated runways of flowers leading into the building. They have staff on site, expert manicurists, and makeup artists who apply makeup to make you look more life-like, almost alive. They have paid barbers and beauticians to make sure that your hair is perfect. People come from miles around just to see you, and they all say nice things about you. You are then laid on a plush bed in a polished coffin with ornate handles and beautifully decorated interiors of angels, doves, and beautiful sunsets.

When it is time for your burial, you are placed in a limousine, and escorted through town by the same police that used to write you tickets. Cars pull over to the side of the street just because you're coming down the road. When you arrive at the cemetery, you don't see dirt from the hole they are about to lower you into because it is covered with fake grass, so it appears that you're not going into the ground.

Finally, they lower you into the ground, not by crude ropes, but by using silver toned wenches. It's beautiful, elegant, and impressive. Still, at the end of the day you are still dead. Sigmund Freud once said,

"People of all cultures are basically convinced of their own immortality." Therefore; death is something that happens to someone else. We attempt to make death look like life.

There is no greater enemy to life than death. Death cancels life. Dr. Manuel Scott once said, "We all are death evaders, but none of us is death escapers." The statistics haven't changed, one of one will die. And when we consider death, we believe that it's all over. But I've got some good news today. Not even time or death can write "finished" over us until God says it's over. Even death has to get God's permission to take us out of here.

1 Corinthians 15:22 For as in Adam all die, even so in Christ shall all be made alive.

Still Waiting on Houdini

Harry Houdini was a Hungarian-American- illusionist and magician. He mesmerized audiences with his very unique ability to escape from handcuffs and shackles. Thousands watched as he was handcuffed, shackled and placed in crates behind closed doors, but in just a matter of minutes he appeared with the chains off. They would chain Houdini and hang him upside down by his ankles and lower his head into a tank of water, but Houdini would escape in front of a sensationalized audience. They would chain him and put him inside a sealed milk barrel and to their amazement he would always free himself. Houdini was so confident in his ability to escape any chain that he said to his wife Bess, that when I died, leave a candle in the window and he would return after death.

Well, old Harry died in 1926 of some mysterious disease, and Mrs. Houdini waited for his return. She waited though 1927, but no return, 1928 no return, 1929 still no Houdini, 1930, 1931, you get the message. If Mrs. Houdini were alive today, she would still be waiting because there is no human in the natural who can break chains of death. There is one who can break every chain even the chain of death. His name is

Jesus Christ.

Revelation 1:18 I am he that liveth and was dead; and, behold, I am alive for evermore, Amen; and have the keys of hell and of death.

Strange Birds

A strange bird wanders into a farmyard one day and the other fowls laugh at it. The ducks wouldn't allow it in their clique, and neither would the chickens. The turkeys thought it was the ugliest bird that they had ever seen. The farmer took the bird in, began to feed it, and it began to grow.

Within months its wingspan was about six feet wide and talons begin to grow on its feet. One day this strange bird flew to the top of the barn and looked up and saw the sun. It sat there for a moment, and after a while it leapt off the barn. It suddenly began to fly towards the sun. Up it went while the other birds watched. This was an eagle that soared to lofty heights. When you are not accepted, laughed at, ridiculed, and ostracized, remember that Christians are strange birds. We are eagles of the Lord.

Isaiah 40:31 But they that wait upon the Lord shall renew their strength; they shall mount up with wings as eagles; they shall run, and not be weary; and they shall walk, and not faint.

Strange Doors

An old farmer from deep in the country of Alabama had never been to a big city before. One summer he decided to take his family to Birmingham for a visit. When he arrived at a beautiful hotel downtown, he and his son walked in to register. He noticed an old woman walking on a cane to a door and pressing a button. The door opened, and a loud bell sounded. The old lady walked in and the doors closed behind her.

The man was amazed because he had never seen an elevator before.

While he stood there watching, the loud bell sounded again, and a beautiful young woman walked out. The old guy turned to his son and said, "Boy, hurry! Go get your maw!"

Genesis 18:10 And he said, I will certainly return unto thee according to the time of life; and, lo, Sarah thy wife shall have a son. And Sarah heard it in the tent door, which was behind him.

Start a Fire

In one of the early shows of "Survivor" the inhabitants were on an island. I noticed the first thing they wanted to do was to start a fire because without fire there would be no warmth. They could not cook their food, and they would have no light at night. Until they could get a fire started, they could do nothing constructive. So it is with the church. If the fire of the Holy Spirit is not in the church, we can do nothing constructive. Start a fire!

Acts 2:3 And there appeared unto them cloven tongues like as of fire and it sat upon each of them.

Storms Reveal Roots

When I returned from a revival in Dallas, Hurricane Irma was over. The remnants of Irma had taken its toll on our neighborhood. As I was running that morning, I noticed that many trees had been uprooted and blown across houses and fences, but there were some trees that were still standing tall and erect. As I was wondering about this, the spirit spoke to me and said, "When storms come, the root is revealed."

Ephesians 3:17 That Christ may dwell in your hearts by faith; that ye, being rooted and grounded in love.

Swearing Grandpa

I was walking out of Ingles the other day, and as I was crossing the cross walk with my groceries, a vehicle driven by an older guy approached. Apparently I was not moving fast enough for him, so he shouted curse words using God's name. Some people have completely given up on God and started cursing His name. Some are using second hand profanity like shucks, dang, darn, and heck, but these are just shortened versions of cursing.

Exodus 20:7 Thou shalt not take the name of the Lord thy God in vain; for the Lord will not hold him guiltless that taketh his name in vain.

Take a Knee

I was watching a movie the other night entitled, "After Earth," with Will Smith and his son Jaden. In the movie, the space craft they were traveling on crashed and Will Smith, who plays the role of father, suffered a severely broken leg. He told his son that the only way for them to survive was for him to go and retrieve a beacon and bring it back to the crippled space craft. Kitai, who was played by Jaden, was afraid to venture outside of the ship, but he got encouragement from Cypher, his father. He said two things to him that got my attention. He told him, "Fear is not real. Danger is. Fear is a choice."

Kitai goes to retrieve the beacon and contracts a loathsome disease in the forest and Cypher, who is watching his frightened son on a monitor, tells him to "Take a knee." This spoke to me because I saw in my sermonic eye something that Jesus tells his children.

Jesus never told his disciples that danger is unlikely. He actually told them quite the opposite. "Behold, I send you forth as sheep in the midst of wolves: be ye therefore wise as serpents, and harmless as doves." Matthew 10:16. Then he told them that because there was imminent danger, they must pray to the Father. "And he spake a parable unto them to this end, that men ought always to pray and not to faint." Luke 18:1 When danger is encircling believers, we must learn to "take a knee."

1 Thessalonians 5:17 Pray without ceasing.

Taking Your Eyes Off the Road

I was traveling north on Clemson Boulevard and came upon a horrible accident. A small Corolla had crashed into the back of a very expensive SUV. There was a young lady standing at the curb with blinding tears, obviously distraught and remorseful. The culprit? Texting. Texting is the most alarming distraction when operating a vehicle. Sending or reading a text that takes your eyes off the road for five seconds, at 55 mph is like driving the length of an entire football field with your eyes closed. You cannot drive safely unless the task of driving has your full attention.

Every one of us who is a child of God has been assigned a journey. On this journey we are guided by GPS (God's Positioning System) to our destiny. Often, we are distracted and disrupted because we take our eyes off the road. Sometimes it's because of a text.

Proverbs 5:21 For the ways of man are before the eyes of the Lord, and he pondereth all his goings.

Taste and See For Yourself

An American atheist society was having a conference in a hotel in a small city. The keynote speaker had been delivering tenets of the doctrine against the faith community. He had bantered on about how religion soils the conscience of the American public and had foisted discrimination against freethinkers. While he was maligning Christianity, there was a hotel maid passing through with a wad of sheets in her arms headed to the washroom. She overheard this man talking boldly against the God of her salvation, and she waited patiently to see what else he had to say.

When he had finished speaking, she walked slowly to the front of the room and every eye was on her, as they wondered what she was about to do. She asked, "How can you be sure of your belief that God does not exist?" The man said, "Have you ever smelled, seen, tasted touched, or heard God?" Her response was, "No." The man continued, "Then your five senses testify that God does not exist?"

The old gray-headed woman laid the sheets down, reached across the desk, and picked up one of the oranges in a bowl on the table. She carefully peeled the orange while the on-lookers wondered what she could be doing. Then she quartered the orange and took a segment of it, and began to eat it in front of the group. She looked at the man and said, "How does this orange taste?" The irate man said, "How would I know? It's in your mouth. You're eating it!" The woman said, "You're right. I tried it, so I know how it tastes. It's good!" The psalmist said, "Oh taste and see that the Lord is good!" What happens to us in life may not be good to us, but it is always good for us because the Lord is good.

Psalms 34:8 O taste and see that the Lord is good: blessed is the man that trusteth in him.

Tater People

Some people are very bossy, and like to tell others what to do, but don't want to spoil their own hands. Too many chiefs and not enough Indians. They are called "Dick Taters." Some people never seem motivated to participate, but are just content to watch while others do the work. They are called "Speck Taters." Some people never do anything to help, but are gifted at finding fault with the way others do the work. They are called "Comment Taters." Some people are always looking to cause problems by asking others to agree with them. It is too hot or too cold, too sour or too sweet. The preaching is too loud and long. Services are too long. They are called "Agie Taters." There are those who say they will help, but somehow just never get around to actually doing the promised help. They give lip service to the Kingdom of God and the Church. They are called "Hezzie Taters." Some people can put up a front and pretend to be someone they are not by being hypocritical. They are called "Emma Taters." Then there are those who love and do what they say they will. They are always prepared to stop whatever they are doing, and lend a helping hand. They bring real sunshine into the lives of others. They are called "Sweet Taters." (Author unknown)

1 Corinthians 12:27 Now ye are the body of Christ, and members in particular.

Technology Can Be A Distraction

When I was a boy, one day of the week at our house was called "washday." On this day, Mom spent the whole day washing clothes. She mad a fire around the wash pot. Then she took a galvanized wash tub and rub board to wash that week's clothes.

Today we have washing machines that have cut the time to a fraction. But what do we do with that extra time? We fill it with something else. It's the same with communication. We used to sit down and write letters, but now we have email. But what we do with the extra time? We fill it with something else. One man walked up to the ticket counter at the airport and asked how long it took to fly from NY to Dallas. The agent who was busy said, "Just a minute." And the guy said thanks and walked off.

We have added speed and noise to our world, but are we any better? Take some time to do something today that has eternal consequences.

Matthew 14:23 And when he had sent the multitudes away, he went up into a mountain apart to pray: and when the evening was come, he was there alone.

Tell God About Your Duck

Two brothers lived on a farm and the younger of the two was throwing rocks one day and accidentally killed one of his dad's ducks. The oldest boy witnessed what happened and threatened to tell their father if he didn't do his chores. One day the oldest brother told the young boy to bring his breakfast to his bed, and the little boy refused. The oldest boy said, "The duck Johnny, the duck." The young boy complied. Again the oldest boy said to the young boy, "Clean my room." The little boy refused. He said, "The duck Johnny, the duck." The little boy got tired and went to his father, and told his father that he had killed one of his ducks. His father told him, "Johnny I saw you when you killed a duck and I was just waiting on you to come tell me about it". The older boy held no more power over him. When we repent, God restores us. Tell God about your duck.

Psalms 32:5 I acknowledge my sin unto thee, and mine iniquity have I not hid. I said, I will confess my transgressions unto the Lord; and thou forgavest the iniquity of my sin.

Tell Him Thank You

When I was a little boy, my uncle Eddie came home to visit. Before he left to go back to New Jersey, he handed me a handful of pennies, and I put them in my pocket. I was so happy that I begin to leap and smile with joy. I began to walk away to go show my friends all the money I had in my pocket. My mama called out to me and said, "Wait a minute, Ronnie, what do you say?" "She said, "Go back and tell your uncle thank you." I never forgot that lesson. The least we can do is tell God, "Thank you."

Philippians 4:6 Be careful for nothing; but in everything by prayer and supplication with thanksgiving let your requests be made known unto God.

Tell Your Story

Fannie Crosby, lyricist, poet, and internationally known hymnist became blind shortly after birth. She never beheld the beauty of the sunrise or the golden glory of a sunset. She never saw a dewdrop twinkle in a lily, and neither did she see a snow blanketed ground on a cold winter morning. She was asked by an interviewer about her blindness, and she responded, "I think God intended for me to be physically blind, so that I might be able to help those see who are spiritually blind." She summed up her life's philosophy in the celebrated hymn, "Blessed Assurance." She penned,

Blessed assurance Jesus is mine,

Oh, what a foretaste of glory divine,

Heir of salvation purchased of God,

Born of his spirit washed and his blood,

This is my story and this is my song,

Praising my Savior all the day long.

We all have a story. Some of our stories are good. Some of our stories are not so good. Some stories are happy. Some stories are sad. Some are filled with depression. Some are filled with delight. Some are filled with happiness. Some are filled with sadness, but we all have stories. We sung in the old church, "Sometimes up, sometimes down, sometimes almost level to the ground."

John 9:24-25 Then again called they the man that was blind, and said unto him, Give God the praise: we know that this man is a sinner. He

answered and said, whether he be a sinner or no, I know not: one thing I know, that, whereas I was blind, now I see.

Thank God Anyhow

A young family sat down to dinner one night and an eight-year-old boy saw that they were having rutabagas and spinach for dinner. The little boy had his mind set on fried chicken but that night they had spinach. His father looked at him and said, "Son, say grace over the meal." The little boy bowed his head and said, "Lord thank you for this food even if we don't want it."

Acts 24: 3 We accept it always, and in all places, most noble Felix, with all thankfulness.

Thanks For the Flowers

The story is told of an old Christian woman who lived beside an evil nonbeliever. The evil neighbor hated the Christian and sought opportunities to prove her disdain for her Christian faith. So every time she cleaned out her chicken coop, she would take the droppings and throw them over the fence into the Christian's yard.

This went on for months, but one day the mean woman became gravely ill, even close to death. She looked up one day and saw the Christian standing by her bed with a bouquet of beautiful roses. She said to the Christian, "I have never seen such beautiful flowers. Where did you get them?" The Christian said, "Do you remember when you would throw those droppings over the fence?" She said, "Yes." The Christian said, "Well, what you didn't know was my flower garden is right next to the fence and you helped fertilize it."

Psalms 110:1 The Lord said unto my Lord, Sit thou at my right hand, until I make thine enemies thy footstool.

Thanksgiving Penney

A pastor noticed that one of his members had not been the church in months, so he decided to pay him a visit. When he arrived, he saw the guy sitting on the porch with a disillusioned look on his face. The pastor greeted him and after a while the conversation moved toward God and the church. The pastor said, "You haven't been to church lately. Is there anything wrong?" Then the man went on a tirade and said, "Why should I come back to church? I've lost my job; my wife has left me for another man; my children went with her, and I haven't seen them in months. To top all of that off, I just left my doctor and he told me that I need a heart operation because my high blood pressure has ruined my arteries. Tell me what do I need to thank God for?"

The wise old pastor went back to his car and brought back a jar with Psalm 116:12 taped to it. What shall I render unto the Lord for all his benefits toward me? He said, I tell you what I want you to do. Over the next two weeks I want you to put a penny in this jar every time you see something God has done for you. Then the pastor left the man's house.

Two weeks later the pastor showed up to the man's home and saw the jar was full of pennies. The man had a big smile on his face. He told the preacher, "Every morning I got out of my bed I had to put a penny in the jar. When I ate my breakfast, I put a penny in the jar. When I strapped on my boots, I had to put a penny in the jar. When I went bed at night, I had to put a penny in the jar. If you think you are not blessed every time you take a breath of fresh air, put a penny in a jar.

Psalms 27:13 I had fainted, unless I had believed to see the goodness of the Lord in the land of the living.

The Devil and Mrs. Job

His wife said to him, "Are you still maintaining your integrity?

Curse God and die!" Job 2:9. Could this be the love of Job's life saying something so foolish? One day Job met this beautiful girl. She was unequivocally stunning. She was absolutely gorgeous, so much so that Job was afraid to ask her out on a date. But he finally mustered up enough nerve and she accepted. One date lead to another and Job discovered that he had slipped down the slippery slope of love to a point of no return. He knew he wanted to marry her so he asked her father for her hand in marriage.

It was a beautiful wedding. Job watched with expectation as she walked down the aisle. The sacred vows were recited and Job and Mrs. Job walked out of the wedding hall the two happiest people in the East. They had humble beginnings, but Job was a consummate businessman and they labored together to make a good life. They brought 10 children into the world as they amassed a fortune together. They became the talk of the town. They were admired, revered, respected by the whole known world as the elite couple in Uz. But one day something happened. They lost it all.

They both sat on the front seat of the chapel surrounded by 10 coffins wherein laid their beautiful children. Everything they had worked for all their lives together was gone--their camels, sheep, oxen and mules, all dead. Job and Mrs. Job were broke. They couldn't file for bankruptcy because there was no such thing. They were miserable. We think often of Job only when we read this book, but we must not leave Mrs. Job out. She loved Job and her children and she suffered along with him. So how could she say such a thing? Was it possible that it wasn't really her that made this stupid statement? I think so.

You see, the devil used Mrs. Job as his mouthpiece. Remember what the devil had told God. He threatened to make Job curse Him to His face. Be careful not to lose your composure when someone you love speaks coarsely to you. It may not be them. It could be the devil using them.

Job 1:11 But put forth thine hand now, and touch all that he hath, and he will curse thee to thy face.

181

The World Is Watching

It seems to me every time God gives me a sermon he allows me to live it out first. Whenever I am preparing a sermon on faith, God presents me with an opportunity to exercise my faith. When I'm preparing to preach on giving, God allows me to face and opportunity to give. Invariably, when I'm called to preach on temptation, I am faced with temptation of some sort.

I was getting ready to preach on how to control your emotions when people and things are getting on your nerves and believe me I had an opportunity to experience it. I was preaching in Newark, New Jersey and we had a very spiritual uplifting and transformational revival. The morning I left the hotel and headed to the airport, my driver got lost in traffic even though his GPS was functioning properly.

When I arrived at the airport, I noticed that there was a line about 50 yards long at check-in. Needless to say, a few of my nerves were lost. When I arrived at security, there was a sister who obviously did not get a good night's rest the night before who had a serious attitude. I lost a few more nerves. I hate flying with a passion, but I'm forced to do it many times a year. This particular day it appeared that it was going to be a good flight because there were few clouds in the sky. I assumed that it would be a good ride from Newark to Charlotte, but how wrong I was. It was the worst flight I had all year. It was a bumpy ride with the captain not giving any warnings as to what was going on.

Finally we arrived in Charlotte and I went to baggage claim to collect my belongings. I was the first to arrive at baggage claim, and I watched as bags went round and round on the conveyor belt. Out of the 200 or more people on the plane everybody grabbed their bag and walked away and I was still looking up in the baggage shoot waiting on mine to arrive. Finally it dawned on me that my bag was not coming down the shoot.

I walked over to baggage claim supervisor and said to her, "My bag is missing." This must've been the same sister that I left in Newark because they were exactly alike. I used all of the self-calming techniques I could muster not to explode, including pulling my cell phone out staring at it to keep from saying anything. When I pulled my cell phone out, she pulled hers out and started texting right in front of me. I lost a bundle of nerves.

I left the airport fuming and just as I exited to get on 85, there was traffic backed up for miles. I had one nerve left. The Holy Spirit reminded me of some basic principles of the Christian faith. We are ambassadors. We represent Christ, and we should be examples of love, faith, hope, and patience. The world is checking out our dispositions, attitudes and demeanor, and too many of us are misrepresenting the faith by going postal and bringing blight on the kingdom.

People are not interested in Churchanity. They are interested in our behavior in the face of stress, trial, and trouble. People are not interested in how high we jump but how straight we walk when we come down. The benediction of every service is nothing, but an opportunity to apply what you heard in the sermon. This was a test for me and a reminder that the world is watching our reaction to disappointment and trouble. We are Disciples of Christ, and he said by our loving attitudes for each other men will know that we are his Disciples.

1 Timothy 4:2 Let no man despise thy youth; but be thou an example of the believers, in word, in conversation, in charity, in spirit, in faith, in purity.

Tree Shakers and Fruit Gatherers

When I was in high school I picked peaches during the summer for $.20 a bushel. I had a friend who worked with me named Wade and we had a system that worked for us. Wade would go up in the tree, shake the tree, and the ripe peaches would fall to the ground. I would pick the peaches up from the ground and put them in the basket. Wade did most of the work I simply gathered the results of his work. In life we have tree shakers and fruit gathers.

Many of us are reaping the benefits of someone who shook the tree. You didn't get your degree on your own. People had to die for that. The Supreme Court decision of Brown versus Board of Education in 1954 came with a lot of resistance. That flag on the Statehouse did not come down easily. Nine people gave their lives for that. Never forget the tree shakers when you are picking up the fruit.

1 Timothy 5:17 Let the elders that rule well be counted worthy of double honour, especially they who labour in the word and doctrine.

Troubling Rocks

There was a little boy riding down the road on his bike with a little boat. He decided to sail his boat on a lake by the road and somehow the boat drifted out in the water. He felt like he had just lost his precious boat and didn't know what to do. Then it dawned on him that he could cast rocks just beyond the boat to create waves and ripples so that the waves would drift the boat back in his direction. He began to cast rocks just beyond the boat and pretty soon the little boat drifted back to the seashore to the little boy's loving hands. Sometimes the Lord will cast rocks at us to bring us closer to Him.

Acts 9:5 And he said, Who art thou, Lord? And the Lord said, I am Jesus whom thou persecutest: it is hard for thee to kick against the pricks.

Trusting Daddy To Catch Me

When I was a little boy, my dad will come home from work and I would be so glad to see him. Often he would reach down and pick me up and throw me up in the air. He was about 6'3" tall, and his arms were close to four feet long. When I left his hands I was at least 13 or 14 feet off the floor, but I would laugh, flay my arms, and tell him to do it again. That's the faith of a child.

Psalms 11:1 In the Lord I put my trust: how say ye to my soul, Flee as a bird to your mountain?

Trusting God for Strength

In lifting weight one must put more weight on the muscles than one can handle to improve strength, it is called the overload principle. I lift weight occasionally, and often I use a spotter. A spotter stands over me just in case I can't lift the weight that is on the bar. God often puts more weight on the bar than we can handle, but He stands over us to make sure we lift it. We get stronger by lifting the weight.

Isaiah 35:3 Strengthen ye the weak hands, and confirm the feeble knees.

Trusting God When the World is Shaken

A terrible earthquake occurred in San Francisco in 1906 that leveled buildings and destroyed bridges and homes. An elderly man was trapped under rubble and when the rescue workers arrived they dug the man out of the debris. To their amazement, the old man was smiling. One rescue worker asked him, "What are you smiling about?" He responded, "I have a God who can shake up the world."

Psalms 18:7 Then the earth shook and trembled; the foundations also of the hills moved and were shaken, because he was wroth.

Trust the Director

In the movie, "Karate Kid 2," Dre Parker who is played by Jaden

Smith, leaves Detroit and flies to Beijing with his mother to live. Dre finds himself encountering bullies on the street of Beijing. When an altercation occurs between some thugs on the street, a Kung Fu master comes to his aid. Han becomes Dre's Kung Fu instructor and Dre finds himself in a tournament. His opponents are much older than him. They are also much larger and they have more experience than he does. At the end of the movie he wins the tournament and gives the credit to his trainer and teacher, Han.

Many of us went to that movie and left saying, "That is impossible." If you notice when the credits rolled, it listed Jaden's father, Will Smith as the producer. When your father produces and writes the movie, nothing is impossible. Our father wrote the script and he directs our story. Whatever you're facing today, God has already written the script and He alone knows the outcome. So, be patient until the credits roll.

Isaiah 40:22 It is he that sitteth upon the circle of the earth, and the inhabitants thereof are as grasshoppers; that stretcheth out the heavens as a curtain, and spreadeth them out as a tent to dwell in.

Trust the Engineer

An old woman boarded a train and was going to visit her daughter in another state. There was a man seated next to her who suffered from claustrophobia. He said, "I am so afraid of closed spaces that I have fainting spells." The lady sat patiently knitting while the train tore into the wind traveling down the track. Just ahead, there was a tunnel that was dark and seemed endless as they began to travel through it. The man was sweating profusely. His heart raced as he told the old woman, "I am about to pass out, what can I do?" The old lady responded, "Mister, you can't jump off this train. Neither can you get a refund on your ticket. Your only option now is to trust the engineer."

Zephaniah 3:12 I will also leave in the midst of thee an afflicted and poor people, and they shall trust in the name of the Lord.

Truth is Narrow

Dr. E.K. Bailey says that he was preaching a revival in a certain city and at the end of his sermon, a well-dressed, well-groomed young man came up to him. The young man said to Dr. Bailey, "You mentioned in your sermon that Jesus is the only way to God, and I think that's very narrow." Dr. Bailey said to the young man, "First of all let's get it straight, I didn't say it, the Bible said it." Then he asked the young man, "What is your profession?" The young man said, "I'm a doctor." Dr. Bailey said, "Let me ask you a question, when you write a prescription for a patient, do you just write down anything?" The young doctor said, "No, I prescribe the medicine that's necessary to heal the patient". Dr. Bailey then said, "You know why you do that? It's because truth is narrow." Dr. Bailey continued, "Have you ever flown on the plane?" The erudite gentleman replied, "Yes." Dr. Bailey said, "When that plane landed, did it land on the interstate, or in a corn field or a parking lot?" "No," was the answer. Dr. Bailey then said, "Do you know why? It is because truth is narrow."

John 14:6 Jesus saith unto him, I am the way, the truth, and the life: no man cometh unto the Father, but by me.

Waiting on Daddy

An old widower had a handicapped son and lived in the backwoods of Alabama. He took his son with him when he went into town to buy groceries and supplies for his farm. One day he took his son with him into town and left him on the wagon because it would have been difficult to take him off the wagon. He said, "Stay here son until I get back. I'll be back in a while."

While the old man was in the store, it became increasingly hot. It was close to 100 degrees and people were walking by and feeling sorry for the little guy on the wagon in the hot sun. One man walked up and said to him, "Let me help you down off that wagon so you can sit over here in the shade by this oak tree." The little boy said to him, "Thank you Sir, but I'm waiting on my daddy." Soon, a lady came by and begged the boy to come down off the wagon to get out of the sun. The lad said, "Thank you ma'am. I'm waiting on my daddy." Another man walked by and said to him, "You're really silly to sit on that wagon as hot as it is. You are going to get heat stroke and sun burn. Why don't you let me help you down so you can sit in the shade? The little fellow said, "No, Sir I'm waiting on my daddy!" It always pays to wait on our heavenly Father.

Psalms 27:14 Wait on the Lord: be of good courage, and he shall strengthen thine heart: wait, I say, on the Lord.

Walking with God

There is an interesting verse in Genesis 5:24, "And Enoch walked with God: and he was not; for God took him." It is said that one day a little girl came home from Sunday school after reading this verse and asked her grandmother what it meant. The wise old mother decided she would answer the question so the little girl could understand it.

She told the little girl that God and Enoch were the best of friends, and God would often visit Enoch every day. Each day when God left Enoch's house, Enoch would walk part of the way home with God. One day when God was leaving Enoch's house, Enoch began asking God about His creation. He asked God how He created the heavens, and God began to explain how He did it. They kept walking. Enoch asked God how He fashioned the stars and the moon, and they kept walking.

The conversations and fellowship were so sweet that ahead they could see the top of God's house and when Enoch looked back, he couldn't see his own house. And God said to Enoch, "Come go home with me. Don't worry about shoes; I've got some golden shoes for your feet. Don't worry about clothes; I've got a long white robe for your back. Don't worry about a hat; I've got a starry crown for your head. Don't worry about a house; I've got a mansion with many rooms for you to live in. Don't worry about light. My Son will light your mansion forever."

Genesis 5:24 And Enoch walked with God: and he was not; for God took him.

Wasteful Christians

If a man lives to be 70 years old and eats two eggs a day, he would eat 51,100 eggs in his life-time. If that same man drinks eight glasses of water containing 8 oz. each, he will drink 12,775 gallons of water. Think of the pigs that would have to die to give him bacon. God is not a God of waste.

There were many non- producing Christians at the church of Corinth that Paul rebuked because of their carnality. They even abused the Lord's Supper. God will always judge us for being wasteful of our time, energy, and our gifts. It behooves us to get busy and be good stewards over the Lord's heritage.

1 Corinthians 11:29-30 For he that eateth and drinketh unworthily, eateth and drinketh damnation to himself, not discerning the Lord's body. For this cause many are weak and sickly among you, and many sleep.

Wearing a Good Name

A young man was arrested for breaking into someone's car. He was taken to jail. When he was being booked, they discovered that he had been arrested on several others occasions for, breaking and entering, public drunkenness, DUI, and disturbing the peace. He was brought before the judge the next day for a hearing and to be arraigned.

When the judge looked at his arrest sheet he was shocked because the young man's name was the same as his. He said to the young man, "You are carrying a good name, but you are not living up to its standards. Every time you commit a crime you bring shame to the name. Because you have my name I'm going to be lenient with you and give you an opportunity to make restitution. I'm doing this because you are carrying my name.

Psalms 23:3 He restoreth my soul: he leadeth me in the paths of righteousness for his name's sake.

When I Look Back

A pastor was constantly annoyed by an old woman who would stand during his celebrative moment in his sermon and look backwards. He noticed that it always occurred when he began to talk about Jesus. The fact that she turned her back to him frustrated him to no end and finally got to a point that he couldn't take anymore. So one Sunday he met the woman in the vestibule and asked her why she stood and turned her back to him while he was preaching.

She said, "I'm sorry baby. I don't mean any harm, but when I turn around, I'm not snubbing you nor disrespecting you. I turn around because I'm looking back to see where the Lord has brought me. He brought me through this. He brought me through that, and every time I turn around there's another blessing."

2 Samuel 22:29-31 For thou art my lamp, O Lord: and the Lord will lighten my darkness. For by thee I have run through a troop: by my God have I leaped over a wall. As for God, his way is perfect; the word of the Lord is tried: he is a buckler to all them that trust in him.

When the Bottom Falls Out

Years ago, when our kids were young, we took them to Six Flags Over Georgia. There was a ride called the Drop Tower, which at first glance, looked like a good idea to ride. I decided to take a chance and bought a ticket, excluding the kids, because you must be a certain age and height to board it. Everyone was strapped in securely and we slowly ascended up a pole, which appeared to be hundreds of feet straight up. There were fifty or sixty people, arranged in a circle around the pole who accompanied me on the ride.

When we arrived at the top, I could see miles and miles east of I-20 Interstate and miles west of I-20. To the north, I could see the skyline of the city of Atlanta, even some of the sky scrapers were visible. As far as my eyes could see were beautiful clouds, flying jets leaving Hartsfield Airport, and the hazed shimmer of mountains back towards the Blue Ridge Parkway. Just as I was enjoying the beauty of the majestic landscape of Atlanta, all of a sudden the bottom fell out. We free fell hundreds of feet in a matter of seconds. People, who had just had lunch, lost it. There were loud thunderous screams, while others shouted with exuberant exhilaration. Some people cried and others appeared stoic and dazed with fear.

When I got back to planet Earth, the Lord spoke to me and said, "Life can be the same way as this amusement ride." Since then, I've discovered the truth of that prophecy.

Job1:19-22 And, behold, there came a great wind from the wilderness, and smote the four corners of the house, and it fell upon the young men, and they are dead; and I only am escaped alone to tell thee. Then Job arose, and rent his mantle, and shaved his head, and fell down upon the ground, and worshipped, And said, Naked came I out of my mother's womb, and naked shall I return thither: the Lord gave, and the Lord hath taken away; blessed be the name of the Lord. In all this Job sinned not, nor charged God foolishly.

When You Can't See God's Hand Trust His Heart

One evening before dinner a young father assembled his family around the dinner table and asked his little girl to pray. The little girl blessed the food and concluded her prayer by saying, "Lord, please don't let mother lose her job. If she loses her job we will not have food to eat. If she loses her job we would not have a home to live in. If mother loses her job we will not have clothes to wear." The young father could hardly wait until she finished her prayer so that he could correct her. All this little girl had ever seen was her father taking her to school and then going back home. She had seen other fathers bring their children to school and then go on to work but her father always went back home. She did not realize that her father worked out of his home because he was a service representative of a large company.

When the little girl finished praying, the young father said, "Sweetheart, the food that we are eating? Your mother did not buy it, I did. The house we are living in? I pay the mortgage. The clothes you're wearing came from money that I earned. You see, Honey, I work upstairs out of my office, and I work every day." This little girl was guilty of only seeing what was obvious to her. Even when we can't see the hand of God, we must trust His heart.

Isaiah 26:4 Trust ye in the Lord forever: for in the Lord Jehovah is everlasting strength.

Where Was God?

A preacher gets a call in the middle of the night that one of his member's sons has been in an accident. He rushes to the hospital and when he arrives, he approaches the emergency room, but finds the young man's mother standing at the door weeping. The young mother looks at the preacher and says, "Preacher, don't come here with that God stuff, now, I can't handle it because my son has just died." The preacher out of concern said, "I just want to have prayer with you. The mother says, "Prayer! Where was God when my son died?" The preacher said, "He's in the same place he when His son died."

When Jesus died, the Bible says that the sun went out and there was total darkness from the sixth to the ninth hour. After he died, the sun rose again. Weeping may endure for a night, but joy will come in the morning. There will be a Friday, but there will also be a Sunday morning. There will be a crucifixion, but there will also be a Resurrection. There's going to be some darkness, but behind every dark cloud the sun will shine.

Psalms 30:5 For his anger endureth but a moment; in his favour is life: weeping may endure for a night, but joy cometh in the morning.

Who is to Blame?

On February 1992, Stella Liebeck ordered a cup of coffee from McDonalds. Liebeck was sitting in the passenger seat of her nephew's car. While removing the cup's lid to add sugar, Liebeck spilled her hot coffee, burning her legs. She blamed MacDonald's for making coffee too hot and filed a lawsuit.

In 1992, 23-year old Karen Norman accidentally backed her car into Galveston Bay after a night of drinking. Norman couldn't operate her seat belt and drowned. Her family blamed Honda Motor Company for making a seat belt that wouldn't operate under water, and they, too, filed a lawsuit.

Richard Harris blamed Anheuser-Busch because he had no luck with the ladies and he got sick when he drank beer. He sued the company for false advertisement in 1991. I wish these were just jokes I'm telling, but they aren't. There are thousands of stories like these that are actual cases of people who play the blame game. You see America's favorite game is not Monopoly, nor Scrabble, nor Candy Crush, Farmville, Battleship, Family Feud. It's the blame game. Why do we blame others for our failures? Why do we shirk responsibility?

We are living in an age where people make up their own truth. They call it alternative truth. In God's eye, alternative truth is a lie. Satan is the master of lies. We lie because of our mother and father of the flesh, Adam and Eve.

Genesis 3:12 And the man said, The woman whom thou gavest to be with me, she gave me of the tree, and I did eat.

Who is Your God?

The paramount question to all of us is not whether or not we believe in God. The most important question is: What kind of god do we believe in? The truth of the matter is most people in this world believe in a god of some sort, whether they will admit it or not. Some will say adamantly that they don't believe in God, but yet they worship fiberglass, gold, silver, and wood. In other words they worship things. People worship houses, cars, and even other people. So, the big question is not what whether you believe in God, but what kind of god you believe in? What god do you worship?

Is God's name Apollo? Athena? Atlas? Zeus? Is it Buddha? Is he the force? Is his name Allah? Does God commanded his followers to behead infidels? Did God really tell those men to fly planes into the Twin Towers in New York in 2001? Did God command the Crusades and the Spanish Inquisition? Again, it is not whether or not you believe in God, but what do you believe about God? It is better not to believe in God at all than to believe the wrong thing about God.

If someone asked you to describe your concept of God in one sentence what would it be? If you were asked to condense all of the attributes of God into one word, what would that word be? 1 John 4:8 says, "God is love." God loves us. All of us. God loves the worst of us. You don't have to be good for God to love you. God loved Osama bin Laden. God loved Adolf Hitler. God loved John Wayne Gacy. God loves Al-Qaeda and Isis.

This fact was confusing to the Pharisees. When they saw Jesus sitting down eating with winos, liars, thieves, adulterers and thugs, they questioned whether it was appropriate. In their eyes, one had to do good things for God to care about them. It's a sad truth, but there are people with that same attitude today. How wrong they are. We are valuable because God loves us. He does not love us because we are valuable. God is love.

1 John 4:8 God is Love.

Why Black History?

When I was in seminary, a well-meaning colleague of mine, who happened to be white, asked me one day, "Ronnie, why is it that African-Americans celebrate Black history? With this country being divided by racial tensions, it seems to me that when you place emphasis on one race or culture you offend other cultures. Shouldn't the church serve to ameliorate racial tensions rather than exaggerating the divide by emphasizing black history?" Now, he was my friend and he was not being rude or disrespectful. He simply wanted an answer to his question.

I told him, we celebrate Black history for many reasons, there are three main reasons. First of all, we celebrate Black history to give a sense of worth to the younger generation. Many young people have been indoctrinated to think that there is something wrong with being black. So, during the month of February, we encourage youth to be proud of the fact that God made them black. They have nothing to be ashamed of because we are a proud people. In other words, an attempt is made to remove the stigma that has been placed on the black race.

Secondly, we celebrate Black history because it gives us an opportunity to emphasize the accomplishments and achievements of our forefathers. History as we know it has not been interested in the contributions that have been made by people of African descent.

Therefore, we remind ourselves of the sacrifices that others have made to bring us to where we are today.

Lastly, and more importantly, we celebrate Black history to remember how far God has brought us. Then I shared this verse Moses spoke to the children of Israel.

Exodus 13:3 And Moses said unto the people, Remember this day, in which ye came out from Egypt, out of the house of bondage; for by strength hand the Lord brought you out from this place: there shall no leavened bread be eaten.

Why Do Grooms Wear Black?

A little girl was attending her first wedding with her mom. She was in awe at the decorations, candles, and music. She was thrilled when the bride came walking down the aisle dressed in a flowing wedding gown. She leaned over and asked, "Mom, why is the bride wearing white?" The mother thought for a moment to give a good answer that her daughter would remember. She leaned over and whispered, "The bride is wearing white because white is the color of happiness, and today is the happiest day of her life." The little girl smiled at her, then she frowned and whispered back to her mom, "Then why is the groom wearing black?"

Genesis 29:25 And it came to pass, that in the morning, behold, it was Leah: and he said to Laban, What is this thou hast done unto me? Did not I serve with thee for Rachel? Wherefore then hast thou beguiled me?

Wrong Measuring Rod

A little boy ran to his mother and said in an excited and cheerful tone, "Mom, I am six feet tall!" The curious mom said, "How do you know Bobby?" He said, "Because I measured myself and I am six ruler lengths tall." The mother said, "Let me see the ruler that you used."

The little boy pulled out a six inch ruler out of his back pocket. The little boy used the correct instrument but the wrong standard.

So many times we measure ourselves using the wrong standard. I could say truthfully say that I'm not a bad person. I've never been a bank robber or a murdered people. I'm not a bootlegger or a gambler; I've never sold drugs or maimed anyone or engaged in any form of crime that would land me in prison. When I measure myself against the standards of other men, I come out to look like a very good person. If I measure myself according to men, that is the wrong standard. It would be an entirely different story if I measured my life to the life of Jesus Christ.

People often say I'm not as bad as someone else, but that's the wrong standard. How do we look against the backdrop of the purity of the Lord? When bank tellers are trained, they are taught to study real money not counterfeit money. Being able to detect what real bills look like makes it easy to identify a counterfeit bill. Jesus Christ is the standard of measurement for the believer not a hypocrite.

Isaiah 6:5 Then said I, Woe is me! for I am undone; because I am a man of unclean lips, and I dwell in the midst of a people of unclean lips: for mine eyes have seen the King, the Lord of hosts.

You Are Not Alone

There was a rite of passage practiced among the Cherokee Indians that when a boy was 13 years old he was taken into the forest and left there all night. One father took his son out one evening. He blind folded him and set him on a stump. He told him to sit there all night until daybreak. That night the young boy was terrified when he heard the strange sounds of animals, but he sat still. The howl of coyotes, the growls of bears, and the hissing of serpents were petrifying to the boy all night but he sat still. He felt something crawl across his feet, but he sat still.

That morning his father returned and took the blind fold off the lad. He said in a proud voice, "You made it! The boy recounted the night by saying, "I heard sounds, but I sat still. I felt something cross my feet, but I sat still. I was so scared, but I remembered your voice telling me to stay there." The man said, "You were not alone. I was just a few feet away watching all night protecting you. I was always here with you."

John 14:18 I will not leave you comfortless: I will come to you.

You Have a Story Too

The four Gospels tell four different stories about Jesus. He tells a story that portrays Jesus as a Jew because he is a Jew and he is addressing the Jews. He traces the genealogy of Jesus back to Abraham to prove that Jesus is truly of Jewish descent.

Mark tells us that Jesus was a Savior of immediacy. He describes Jesus as always being on the move. He is constantly working miracles and trying to help people. Mark shows us a busy Christ.

Luke tells the story of the suffering servant because he spends two thirds of his gospel on Passion Week, the week leading up to the crucifixion. Luke wants us to see that our salvation did not come from Family Dollar or Wal-Mart. It costs Jesus dearly to save us.

John tells a story of a loving God who existed in the beginning before the beginning began to be. In the beginning was the Word and the Word was God and the Word was with God. John emphasized seven signs and all of them show a different aspect of the Lord's deity.

Still, there is the gospel according to you, and no one can tell it but you. No one can tell it like you because it's your story. What does Jesus mean to you and who have you told your story lately?

Years ago, there was water around my water heater, and I knew there was a problem. I called a plumber and he gave me some knowledge about the water heaters that caught my attention. He said, "Every water heater has a relief valve to release the pressure of the heater when it gets too hot. If the pressure is not released because of a faulty relief valve, the water heater could explode and cause serious damage to your home or even death." Your story is a relief valve and if you don't tell it, you could explode.

Revelation 12:11 And they overcame him by the blood of the Lamb, and by the word of their testimony; and they loved not their lives unto the death.

You Will Get Out Of It What You Put In It

Many years ago I stepped in the shower and there was no water. I went to the sink and there was no water, and I did not understand what was going on. We had a well pump that was not working, so I called someone I knew that was familiar with wells.

After working on the pump for a while, he discovered that the pump lost prime. He sent me to get a gallon of water, and I brought the water to him. He poured it down in the pump, and the pump started working. Then he told me in order to get water out of the pump I would have to put water into it. In other words, you get out of it what you put into it. We get out of our kids what we put into them.

Psalms 132:12 If thy children will keep my covenant and my testimony that I shall teach them, their children shall also sit upon thy throne for evermore.

You've Swallowed My Sock

You must accept responsibility to make your marriage better. When a couple was preparing to get married, they both realized that they had a problem. The groom-to-be had very smelly feet. He asked his dad for advice. His dad told him to always wear socks to bed. The bride-to-be told her mom that her breath was so bad in the morning that she was afraid her new husband wouldn't want to sleep in the same room with her. Her mom counseled her never to talk in the morning without first brushing her teeth.

They got married and everything went well for about six months because they both followed the advice they were given. That is, until one morning when the husband woke up to find that one of his socks had come off during the night. As he frantically searched the bed, his wife woke up. She was so startled that she questioned him without remembering to brush her teeth. "What on earth are you doing?" she asked. The husband gasped, "Oh no, you've swallowed my sock!"

Ephesians 5:33 Nevertheless let every one of you in particular so love his wife even as himself; and the wife see that she reverence her husband.

www.ingramcontent.com/pod-product-compliance
Lightning Source LLC
Chambersburg PA
CBHW020656030726
47498CB00002B/534